BRUTAL DEMON

PLANET OF KINGS BOOK 5

LEE SAVINO &

TABITHA BLACK

SILVERWOOD PRESS

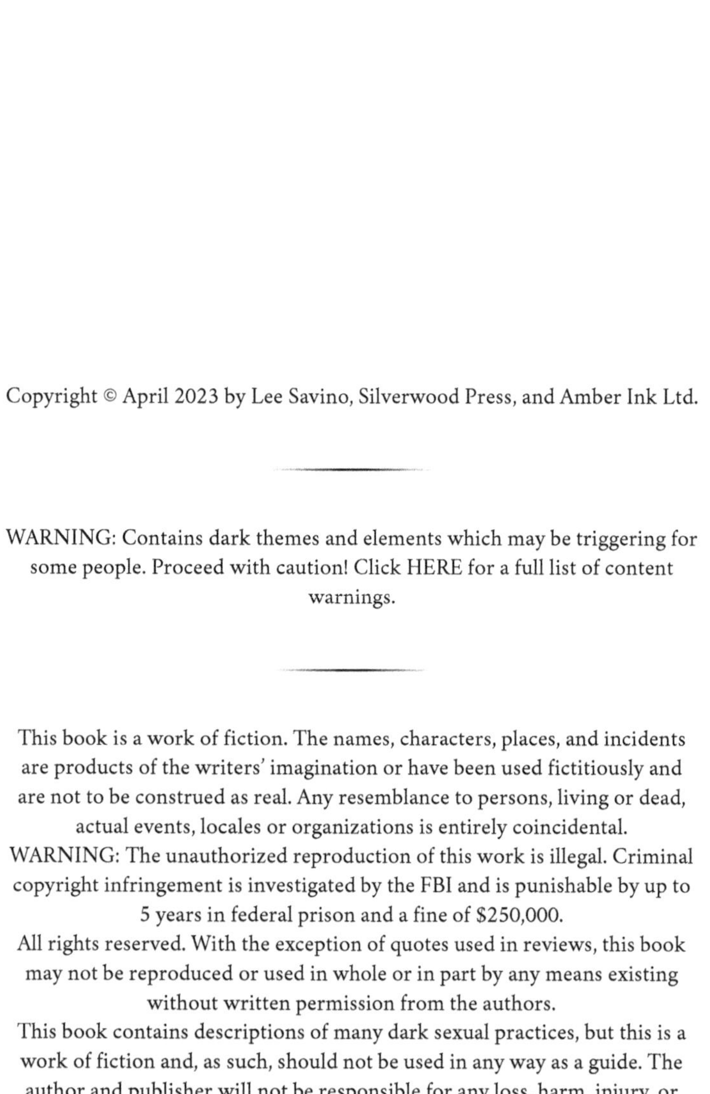

__The Demon King finds a pet...__

When I woke up on a different freaking planet, I was pretty sure my day couldn't get any worse.

I was wrong.

The aliens who found me decided I was sent from heaven and that I should be given to their king — who has a somewhat dubious reputation.

Turns out he's a demon. Of course, he's wicked AF. They don't call him *His Evilness* for nothing.

Before you can say 'hissy fit', I get tied to a tree and left to be sacrificed like some innocent young maiden. Problem is, I'm none of those things.

What if he's disappointed? Then again... what if he isn't?

And when Krav the Demon King comes to claim his waiting gift, I'm not sure which is worse: the way my body responds to him, or the way the feeling seems to be mutual...

CONTENT WARNINGS:

The Planet of Kings books are dark Omegaverse tales with adult themes. Read at your own risk.
Please follow this link for a full list of content warnings for each individual title:
www.leesavino.com/brutal-series-tropes-and-content-warnings/

ONE

Renee

I'VE HAD BETTER DAYS.

For a start, I don't know where I am. Not in the sense of, *I took a wrong turn off I-45 and this neighborhood isn't familiar,* but more like: I woke up in the dirt feeling like I got hit by a truck, and looked up to see three suns blazing in the sky. Three. Freaking. Suns.

It got weirder from there.

I'm dressed in regular clothes—jean shorts, a pretty blue tank with *Not Today, Satan!* emblazoned across the chest—but what I'm wearing is the only familiar thing anywhere near me. I'm dopey, like I took a sleeping pill last night, and as I try over and over again to identify my surroundings, I can't help but wonder whether I'm still dreaming.

Please let me still be dreaming.

Did I hit my head? Because I'm seeing triple. There's no way there are three suns in the sky. The air is smoky like I'm standing on the wrong side of a barbecue. The familiar flat landscape of my backyard is gone, replaced by black, craggy mountains. One of them, the biggest, looms closer than the rest. Its top burns bright red.

Someone is hustling towards me. The figure is very tall, very slender, and very green. And apparently very surprised to see me.

When they speak, it sounds like someone drunk trying to speak a combination of Dutch and Spanish—but somehow, I understand perfectly. "Hello, stranger, are you well?"

I open my mouth to reply. "Not really. I don't know where I am." I'm speaking English, but what comes out is that weird, garbled language. In my voice. I cough and try again. "What the fuck?" Something I suspect might be ash clogs my throat, and I hack it up. I'm not making the best impression, but what can I do?

"You will come with me now." I can tell from her voice that the strange creature is female—albeit well over six feet tall. She beckons and I stumble after her. I'm thirsty as all hell, breathing in the smoke-thickened air, and coughing nonstop. "Poor stranger. I will find you something to drink."

I pick my way over the rocky ground, following as fast as I can in bare feet—god only knows what happened to my shoes. We pass between two giant boulders made of reddish rock. The green woman leads me to a cluster of dwellings beyond. Each building is low to the ground and rounded, made from some sort of stone that reminds me of adobe.

"One moment." My companion ducks her head to dip into the nearest building, and reappears with a cup of something that smells sweet. Is it safe to drink? I'm too thirsty to care.

The liquid is tart and refreshing, and I gulp it down.

"Wait here," my guide says in her strange language, and glides elegantly away.

I stand clutching the empty cup, the suns blazing down on the back of my neck. The village dwellings are arranged around a central circle. The climate is desert dry, and barren aside from some scraggly trees with black trunks. The few plants at my feet have more thorns than needle-like leaves. The air is hot and filled with floating ash, probably because of the giant mountain with the smoking top.

I'm not an expert on volcanoes, but that can't be a good sign.

One by one, the doors to various huts open, and more figures emerge. They don't look like any humans I've ever seen before but I assume the tall ones are adults, and the shorter ones clinging to their robes are children. They cluster around me, dipping close to stare, but staying out of reach.

Three suns in the sky. Unfamiliar surroundings. Crazy tall people who don't look human. Suddenly being able to speak another language. Unwilling to face the conclusion I'm coming to, I shove the thoughts aside.

The green lady returns, parting the crowd. She's accompanied by a crimson figure, who steps in front of her to appraise me.

I blink up at him. He's even taller than the woman, and wearing some weird combination of latex and fur. But it's not his insane height—at least a foot on me, maybe more— or gimpy costume that's the oddest thing about him. His skin is a deep, rich shade of red—the kind you'd love to own in a lipstick—and patterned with pale pink markings, like a tiger or a zebra has on their fur. Oh, and his hair is orange, including his eyebrows, lashes, and wispy chin beard. He's staring at me with ruby eyes, his creased forehead crinkled.

From the reverent way the people behind him are behaving, I can only assume he's some kind of leader to them. A village elder of sorts. And he's obviously deciding what to do with me.

We're facing off in front of the crowd. I have so many questions, I don't know where to begin.

After a long, tense silence, he is the first to speak. "Who are you?"

"I'm Renee. Who are you?"

"Alkarvi. I'm in charge of this settlement."

"It's nice to meet you." I figure it can't hurt to be polite. Taking a deep breath, I ask the question that's been weighing on me since I first opened my eyes and found myself here. "Where are we?"

"This is the settlement Solum, in the Kingdom of Pyreda."

"Uh… right. Okay." I pause a beat, wondering how the heck to phrase my next question without sounding like a fool. "And… er… Pyreda. Can't say I've heard of it. What country are we in?"

He tilts his head. "Country?" he repeats, like it's an unfamiliar concept to him.

"Yeah. See… I'm from Houston, which is in Texas. The United States?"

"Ah. Yes. This is the Kingdom of Pyreda, which is in Ulfaria."

"So this country is called Ulfaria?"

"No. This *planet* is Ulfaria," he corrects me calmly.

There's a sudden swooping feeling in my gut as I try to absorb the magnitude of what I'm being told. So much for avoiding reality. White spots dance in my vision, and I wish there was something nearby I could collapse against. "Planet…" I mumble, my thoughts racing so fast now that I can't keep up with them. *I can't be on another planet.*

"How did you come to be here?" Alkarvi says.

"I don't know. I just… woke up here." I dig my nails into my palms to try and regain control over myself. "My memories are hazy. I think I ate too many mini microwave corn dogs last night and I'm dreaming all this." I *hope* I'm dreaming it.

Alkarvi shakes his shaggy orange head. "No dream," he says. "This is real."

"That's what I was afraid of." I rub my eyes, which are burning from the smoky air.

"Who is she?" someone calls out from the back of the crowd.

For a long moment, Alkarvi stares at me. I can't read his expression at all. At length, he turns to face the people behind him. They're all impossibly tall, and they're all tinted different colors of the rainbow with contrasting, swirling markings on their skin like tattoos.

Aliens. My mind whispers the word but I refuse to listen.

I'm probably in shock.

"Renee, from the Kingdom of Houston," Alkarvi declares. *The Kingdom of Houston*. In any other circumstances, it would be funny. But I'm not laughing right now. There's something in his tone... a new note of authority. "She was sent to us by Ulf himself, and it is clear why."

"Why?" My voice is drowned out by all the others.

"For many, many moon-cycles, Pyreda has suffered. Unlike other blessed kingdoms—Aurum, Altrim, Arboron— we have no content and capable King. Instead, we have a Demon."

The people all murmur what sounds like agreement at Alkarvi's words.

"A Demon who is our king by birthright, but not where it matters: in deed!" The old guy is getting into his stride now, his voice rising, growing more vehement. "Not only does he refuse to be a true leader to us, he actively harms us! And when we ask ourselves why, there is only one answer: Krav The Demon King is displeased with us! Why else would he take our females, especially the young and lovely? Why else would he leave his people to fend for themselves, when Mount Vracor threatens to erupt?" He waves wildly at the volcano, which is steadily belching more thick gray smoke into the air. "He is a monster who never leaves his shadowy castle, and uses the burning lake to keep us away because he finds us so offensive!"

The murmurs of accord are now underscored with jeers, and the occasional squawk of objection.

"By sending this… this…" Alkarvi gestures at me, "Houstonii to us, Ulf is giving us a sign! We must offer her to His Evilness as a symbol of our devotion. As a sacrifice to pacify and please him!"

"Wait, what? A *sacrifice?*" *Demon King* sounds bad. *His Evilness* sounds even worse. I splutter, barely able to find words, but the villagers are beside themselves, shouting, *Praise Ulf!* and stamping their feet. *Ulf* must be a god to them.

"Let us bring him the offering now!" the elder continues, ignoring me.

"I'm not an offering, I'm not a sacrifice, and I'm not a fucking *Houstonii*—whatever the fuck that is!" I yell, sheer panic overcoming any attempt to be polite as I'm rushed by the mob.

Now I know how the witches felt in 17th-century Salem. Everything's a blur as I'm seized and lifted by a bevy of strong hands, and dragged away from the village.

I buck and twist but don't stand a chance against these impossibly strong, rainbow giants. "Please… please let me go," I beg them. "I don't want to be given to a demon."

Not a statement I ever thought I'd say.

Is this shit actually happening? Or have I been roofied with the best hallucinogen known to man? I'm a forty-one-year-old physical therapist from Texas, not a student attending her first *Burning Man* festival.

Peering between the bodies of my captors, I try to get a sense of my surroundings, but everything's flashing past in a blur. With no other option, I go limp and give up the struggle. It's probably better to save my energy for whatever awaits me at the end of this. At least they're not dragging my toes over the rocks.

Eventually, we stop moving and I'm dumped unceremoniously back on my feet. Two of the villagers keep a tight grip on my upper arms, an unspoken reminder that I'm a captive now.

I look around, trying to get my brain to believe what my eyes are seeing. We're a few hundred feet away from the blackened edge of a lake…

An orange, bubbling lake. Steam rises from it in foul-scented clouds, and the searing heat scorches my bare face and legs.

Lava, my brain supplies helpfully. Yeah, thanks for that.

Off in the distance, far beyond the boiling liquid surface, a black turret rises. It's all jagged lines and pointy bits, directly out of a *Tim Burton* movie. In the distance, the volcano—Mount Vracor as they call it—rumbles. Is it getting ready to erupt?

The aliens don't seem to mind the lava lake or their impending Pompeii reenactment. Cheered on by the rest, a small group of them is busy fashioning a stake of sorts out of a nearby tree. Long, supple vines extend from its bare branches, and it doesn't take a rocket scientist to work out what they intend to do with those.

"Hey!" I protest as the two people holding me drag me over to where Alkarvi is standing, stroking his fuzzy beard. "Look," I begin once I'm right in front of him, "I believe this is all a big misunderstanding. I don't think your king—His Evilness, was it?—would be interested in *me*. No, you want a beautiful, twenty-something virgin. While beauty is obviously in the eye of the beholder, I had my first legal beer a couple of *decades* ago. And this might be TMI, but I'm not a virgin… that changed even before the beer. So if you could just let me go—"

"Enough!" Alkarvi snaps, cutting me off, impatience flashing in his ruby eyes. "Ulf has decreed that we offer you to the demon who rules us. King Krav of Pyreda will decide what to do with his gift." He addresses the ones holding me. "Secure her to the *cex*."

"Sex?" I bleat as I'm hauled over to the tree and shoved up against it, the bark scraping my back. "Please, this is a mistake!" The villagers ignore me, holding me down and securing the vines around my waist, ankles, and wrists until they bite into my flesh. "You don't want me. I'm too old. I'm divorced!"

I yank at the bindings, but they hold fast. My captors back away, looking satisfied. The volcano has stopped belching smoke and the wind has cleared most of it away, but the lava lake is blistering hot and bubbling. On the far side of the roiling surface, a bubble pops, and sparks land on a dead tree a few feet away from the lava's edge. The wood catches fire, turning the tree into a merrily burning torch.

"What if the king doesn't come?" I ask Alkarvi, not sure which I'm more afraid of—the Demon King finding me, or being left to die a slow, thirsty death in some weird alien parody of a crucifixion. Not to mention, I'm a redhead. *One* sun is bad enough, but being tied up bare-limbed under *three…*

"He will come," Alkarvi assures me. "We will make sure of that. Ulf desires that Krav receives our gift to him." The tall alien and his acolytes turn on their heels, and leave me alone.

Well, crap. What in the actual blue fuck do I do now?

Krav

We demons cherish our solitude—at least, I do, and I assume it's the same for everyone. My father certainly did.

That's why he built this castle out in the plains, in the shadow of Mount Vracor, as far away from the rabble as possible, and surrounded it with a lava lake. Some kings take great pride in being rulers of the people, sacrificing their time and energy to ensure their kingdoms are healthy and prosperous.

Those kings are fools. The common folk are never grateful, never appreciate what they have. Instead, they always want more. They demand and demand, like *lykka* chicks with their beaks permanently stretched open. My father silenced them by raining fire on their heads, and dropping the occasional village elder into Mount Vracor. Now he's gone, it's my turn to continue his reign of terror. But I barely engage with the Pyredii. Why bother trying to satisfy those who will never be satisfied?

Instead, I concentrate on pleasing myself. My palace might look dark and forbidding from the outside—as intended—but on the inside, I have everything I could want. Sumptuous furnishings, the best wines and food brought in by the *jynx*—my shadow servants—musical instruments to play, and numerous other luxuries. My library alone is filled with more reading material than I could manage in a lifetime.

I do not miss company. When I require companionship, I spend time with Plutus, taking him out for a jaunt. When I wish to satisfy my carnal urges, I don a disguise, and head out to find a pleasure slave. Since they are all Betas, I never need to worry about going into rut, or impregnating them. I slake my dark desires on their willing, supple bodies—if I like them, I ensure they, too, have their satisfaction—and then I leave.

A perfect arrangement.

When I first became king, the Pyredii begged me to be a different kind of ruler than my father. They sent emissaries to petition me, pleading that I visit their villages and bless their hunting parties and their crops. To quiet the rumbling volcano, since Mount Vracor is said to be tied to the king's moods and will, and it spews fire when I am discontent. Or suffering from indigestion.

I scoffed then, as I do now.

Eventually, they gave up. Those who persisted in pestering me learned the hard way not to irritate their king —especially if he happens to be a demon. A few flights over Mount Vracor when it was at its most threatening silenced my people's whining.

Fear is an incredibly powerful tool. A great motivator. The end result was that I was able to enjoy a great number of years of being left alone, in peace, with no one begging, demanding, or requiring anything of me—at least, not in person. I still receive the occasional missive, but they're set aside. Ignored. I have no interest in what the common folk have to tell me.

Until today.

A *jynx* brings me a message from the head of Solum, the village closest to my palace. Apparently, they have a gift for me. An offering. As someone who wants for nothing, who can conjure up almost anything he desires, I am bemused by the notion. Then I hear that since they are too afraid to bring this gift directly to me, I must go and fetch it myself, like some common delivery whelp. My bemusement immediately turns into irritation.

I refuse to be summoned. I send a *jynx* ahead to see what this offering might be, and whether it's worth leaving the comfort of my castle to obtain.

The *jynx* returns and whispers a single word in my ear. Certain I misheard, I ask him to repeat it. And again.

Omega.

The ground shudders. In the distance, Mount Vracor smokes.

"Is that so?" I rise from my chair and begin to pace, the hem of my long cloak sweeping the floor. A while ago, I learned in a Kings' Council meeting that the Stone King had found some way to bring Omegas to Ulfaria, but nobody knew how many there were—or where they could be found, since the magicians had miscalculated and scattered them across the planet. That golden buffoon Aurus merely told me his warriors were searching for the missing females. I never did get an update on that—probably because Aurus only cares about Aurus, and he already has his Omega.

Then I received an invitation from Medela, inviting me to some ball, so it seems King Bestian, too, has found a queen. Since I didn't attend, I don't know whether his new mate is also one of these Hoo-man Omegas, but it's likely.

Could this random gift from Solum truly be an Omega? A real one? I close my eyes, trying to recall every detail of the ones I saw at the council meetings. They all seemed tiny, although the orbs do distort size somewhat. Perhaps I should have bestirred myself to attend in person for once.

Ah well. Too late now.

"Prepare my chambers," I order the *jynx*. "Fresh bedding —oh, and lay out some refreshments fitting for an Omega— whatever Aurus feeds his queen." Just in case this Omega is one of the Hoo-mans the Stone King brought over. The *jynx* can search the magicians' records for more information on suitable food and drink. "I'm off to collect my gift." Unwilling to wait one more moment, I shuck off my cloak and let my wings unfold as I stride to the extra-large window I had built into the wall of my quarters, which are on the upmost levels of the castle. I like to have an exit in every room.

I generally detest surprises, but this one could be interesting.

We shall see.

TWO

Renee

I'VE LOST all sense of time. The suns have shifted slightly, no longer blazing directly onto my bare skin, which I'm grateful for, but I'm still tied to a fucking tree like the bimbo lead in a second-rate horror movie. At least the wind has suppressed the plumes of ash so I can breathe. The smoke trails from the volcano have thinned.

The initial panic has subsided a little, and I've had a lot of time to think. Not sure if that's a good thing. I've tried and tried to remember what I was doing before I fell asleep/passed out/died and went to alien hell, but I just can't. Considering my outfit, I definitely wasn't in bed asleep, nor was I at work. But there are still so many other options…

Shopping, driving, getting a mani-pedi, chilling with a book, getting coffee with a friend… none of them would ordinarily lead to this particular situation. This is real life, after all.

Then again, maybe it's not. Maybe I've managed to teleport myself into some steamy monster romance novel, like an X-rated version of *The Neverending Story*. Lately, my book boyfriends have been more Beast than Prince Charming—minotaurs, orcs, even a Kraken—although I haven't yet tried a demon.

If he shows up, you might get your chance, I think, then tell that cynical, resort-to-humor-in-any-difficult-situation voice to shut the hell up. *This ain't the time for jokes*, as my mom used to say.

God, though, what if he does show up?

What if he doesn't?

I'm pretty screwed either way. There's no guarantee this Demon King won't just kill me. His own people refer to him as *His Evilness*.

"We're not in Kansas anymore, Toto," I say aloud. Maybe I'm having a nervous breakdown, like my Aunt Nettie when her husband upped and left. I used to think that whole *I'm going out to get cigarettes* thing was some kind of urban legend, until it happened to my family. My auntie's husband did just that—told her he was heading to the store, and never came back. He just vanished, like he never even existed. Poof. Gone.

As crappy as Phillip was as a husband, at least he had the decency to *tell* me he wanted a divorce. To stay in communication with me through the whole process. We even still follow each other on social media. And in my darkest days during that separation, when I found myself sobbing in bed in the middle of the night, wondering if that was it for me romantically and I was going to die alone, I often comforted myself with that little thought: at least I was getting closure. Unlike poor Nettie.

Life doesn't give you what you want. You get what you get, and you have to make the best of it. When life gives me lemons, I make margaritas. I prefer them with lime, but lemon is better than nothing.

I would freaking kill for a cocktail right now. My arms are beginning to ache, spread-eagled as I am, and I'm getting groggy. Dehydration? Or just exhaustion? How long have I been tied up here? What is *exposure*, anyway? You hear of people getting lost out in the wilderness and dying of exposure. Is that the same thing as dying of hunger and thirst? Does everyone have constant random thoughts, or is it just me?

The ground rumbles beneath my tied feet. The lake pulses like it's going to slop over its edges. I shrink back against the tree, praying the lava doesn't flow towards me.

Lava, volcanoes, and now earthquakes. Is this hell, or purgatory? Definitely isn't heaven.

At least I'm not tied to the top of the volcano. It's hard enough to breathe down here.

The mini-quake subsides, and the lake's surface has resumed its former rolling boil. A cool breeze whispers over my face.

Goosebumps prickle over the skin of my arms and legs. I squint across the bubbling expanse of the lake to the gothic-looking turret beyond.

A shadowy shape emerges from the tower and hurtles over the lake. My heart stops.

It's approaching me—fast. And as it gets closer, my panic increases. It's big… no, it's freaking *huge*.

A monster.

The Demon King?

It's flying on massive, black, bat-like wings, heading straight towards me.

Please faint, I beg myself. *Please, please, please. Just pass out… now*. But I remain agonizingly conscious. As soon as I can make out the curved horns, I do the next best thing, and squeeze my eyes shut. *Please go away*, I pray. I may not be a twenty-year-old virgin, but I'm still definitely too young to die.

There's a gust of air over my bare skin and, even with my eyes shut, I can tell when the shadow falls over me. He's close enough to block out the light, like when the sun goes behind a huge cloud.

A deep, rasping growl makes the hairs on the back of my neck rise and bizarrely, out of nowhere, a bolt of lust shoots through my lower belly.

I'm hit with the most delicious, decadent scent—leather, bitter chocolate, cigars in a humidor, with an underlying note of something musky I can't place—and an urgent, liquid heat surges between my legs with such ferocity, I let out a gasp.

"Look at me," a voice rasps. It's not a request. It's a command.

Keeping my eyes squeezed shut, I give the barest shake of my head. I can't look. I'm too terrified. Too inexplicably turned on.

"I command you to look at me!" The raspy voice is now a roll of thunder which renders me incapable of disobedience. My heart is thumping in time with my clit.

My eyes fly open, and I meet the demon's gaze. His pupils are black slits in a sea of mystic topaz. I'm drowning in his eyes, unable to look away.

What the fuck is happening to me?

"Omega," he growls, and there's another rush of desire between my legs. I arch my back as need rolls through me. Something wraps around my leg and cinches tight. "Mine."

"I'm not—" I manage to squeak before his lips land on mine in a kiss that sears my soul. His tongue is in my mouth, possessing, demanding, and I'm drowning in the heady, smoked chocolate taste of him. His scent is overwhelming now, surrounding me like a tangible cloud. There's a clenching in my lower belly like I haven't felt since I was a teenager with my first boyfriend.

I should pull away, tell him to stop this immediately, give him a long lecture about consent...

I do none of those things. Instead, I arch up and kiss him

back with all the hungry desire he's invoking in me. Desperate to touch him, I curse the vines holding my wrists in place.

The yearning, liquid ache between my thighs is growing stronger by the second.

When I'm about to black out from lack of air, he pulls away just the slightest bit. His face is still too close for me to see properly.

I gulp in a breath, dazed and trembling, trying to make sense of my reaction to him.

The demon lets out a growl, but instead of fear, heat blooms in me. The muscles in my core tighten, and my lust ratchets up a thousand percent. "Omega," he snarls again, and before I can ask him what the hell that means, he reaches out and shears my shorts and panties off my body with a single black talon.

Oh fuck. Oh fuckfuckfuck…

The vines around my ankles and waist are the next victims of his razor-sharp claws, leaving me dangling by my wrists, naked from my belly button down.

He hasn't stopped growling. The sound vibrates through every fiber of my body, making me hum like a tuning fork.

My pussy is soaked, my arousal dribbling down the insides of my thighs. I may not know what I want, but my body is in no fucking doubt.

The demon once again slants his mouth over mine, kissing me in a way I've only ever read about, and it feels so good that I never want him to stop.

If this is a dream, it just got ridiculously good.

The tight grip around my calf eases. There's a sharp clack like a flick-knife being opened, then his huge, hot hands are on my bare butt, cupping my cheeks, pulling me up and towards him. Since there's no searing pain, he must have retracted his claws.

I part my thighs willingly, hooking my legs around his

hips. All I can think about is satisfying the throbbing need in my clit. In fact, I would be begging him right about now if his lips weren't still on mine, his tongue driving me damn near out of my mind.

The demon's skin is smooth but tough and burning hot, like he's possessed by fever. I thought I was boiling before, but that was nothing compared to now, in the presence of this monster who radiates heat like an Aga oven.

Something huge and blunt brushes against my sex, and for the first time since the demon first kissed me, a shard of panic slices through my lust. That can't be his cock. It has to be his knee. It's too big, it's—

Impossible, I think in a daze as the tip slides between my slick pussy lips, stretching me to the point of burning. And yet even despite the sharp ache, the pulsing thump in my clit intensifies and I find myself wanting to take all of him.

I want this demon to fuck me.

As if he can read my mind, he lets out a roar and thrusts hard, driving my whole body back against the tree. With his hands still gripping my ass, protecting my bare skin from the bark, he holds me in place like a rag doll and proceeds to pound me with long, firm strokes.

I'm being split in half by a monster, my thighs are aching from being stretched around his bulky waist, the vine-bonds are chafing my wrists…

…and yet it's the most thrilling, heady, intense experience of my life.

Still kissing me, he tilts his pelvis, changing the angle so my stiff, swollen clit is getting the friction I'm so desperate for. Not three strokes later, I'm coming, rolling waves of pleasure starting in my core and pulsing through my whole body. I want to scream, want to grab his shoulders, grip his arms, something—but since my hands are still tied and his mouth is still crushing mine, all I can do is surrender, riding out my orgasm until it at last begins to ebb.

Either the demon doesn't notice or doesn't care that I just climaxed; he just keeps on pounding me, pulling almost all the way out and thrusting back in, hard, his pelvis rhythmically crushing my now over-sensitive clit. Wriggling with the discomfort, I slant my head, trying to break the kiss. I want to tell him to change his angle but my protests are muffled by his lips and tongue as he steps up the pace, fucking me harder now.

I can't believe how wet I am.

To distract myself from the uncomfortable sensations in my most sensitive spot, I focus on the way his cock feels inside me, filling me completely with each measured, controlled thrust. Every time he goes in, something rubs hard against a place deep inside me and it feels so damn good, I want to weep with the intensity of it. It's like the demon's cock has a built-in G-spot stimulator, and I'm here for it.

Then there's a new, searing burn where our bodies are joined. If I didn't know better, I'd say his dick just got a whole lot thicker, stretching my pussy like a fist. Weirdly, the sharp ache goes straight to my clit, replacing the hyper-sensitivity with renewed pleasure. The demon tenses and rears up, breaking our kiss with a roar that makes my whole body shudder. Clutching me to him with his hands still on my ass-cheeks, he gives a couple mini thrusts, and roars again.

I can feel him jerking inside me, filling me up with each pulse, and it's so raw and primal that I'm just about ready to come again. My pussy flutters around him and I groan at how good it feels.

Please don't stop now, I beg silently. *Please. Just give me a little more…*

But the demon has stilled. For a long moment, he simply stands there, still inside me, my legs still wrapped around him. I shift, and my bare calf brushes against what can only be his tail, yanking me back to reality with a jolt. I cast around for something to say, and come up empty.

That doesn't happen often.

With a grunt, the Demon King—I assume, since we still haven't been formally introduced—grips my hips and yanks himself out of my throbbing pussy. The stab of pain makes me gasp.

"There, there, little Omega," he says, his voice like cascading rocks, "the ache will fade soon."

His tone has a soothing note. I blink, wondering if I heard right. Is he patronizing me? Or is he a closet Daddy-Dom? And what's an *Omega*?

This isn't what I expected from *His Evilness*. At least I'm not dead.

He smoothes my damp hair back from my face, careful not to slice me with his freaky black talons. Thank god he can retract them. His touch is gentle for a creature with a giant frame and black horns. Even his tail—long and thick and the same color as the rest of him—strokes my hip with the same tenderness he's using to touch my face.

I whimper as he removes my legs from around his waist and returns my feet to the ground, steadying me with his hands and tail. There's a rush of liquid between my thighs and I glance down to see his cum dripping out of me. It looks like there's cupfuls of the lavender-tinted stuff, but that can't be.

"I'm Renee," I croak, my voice hoarse from thirst and lack of use. "Are you—"

"The Demon King," he replies, extending a terrifying talon and slashing the vines off my wrists. As soon as I'm untied, I lose my balance and sway. The next moment, he scoops me up into his massive arms and cradles me against his chest. His skin is the color of plums, with pale bronze markings. I look up at him, trying to take in every detail.

Gleaming, thick black hair tumbles over his shoulders

and frames an expansive, chiseled face crowned by two impressive, dual-pronged horns. Everything about him is wide, from his sleek, slanted eyebrows to his generous mouth. His neatly groomed goatee is twisted into three little braids, each adorned with bronze beads. Lifting my gaze higher, I take in his broad, slightly flat nose, and make myself meet his eyes.

The Demon King has the most incredible irises— glittering like multicolored gemstones—enhanced by thick, deep violet lashes I'm immediately envious of. But it's the way he's looking at me that makes my tummy twist and another slow thump of desire pulse between my legs. I always thought of myself as demisexual, unable to be sexually attracted to anyone without an emotional connection.

Guess I was wrong.

"Renee," he murmurs, and his tone sends shivers of pleasure skittering down my spine. "A true Omega. My Omega. The *jynx* was telling the truth."

Omega? Jynx? I have no idea what he's talking about but I guess it's time to set the record straight—before he gets me so riled up again I can't resist him. "I'm not your… anything," I begin, still taken aback by the way my words get jumbled into his language every time I speak. "I appreciate that I may have given you the wrong impression just now, and don't get me wrong, it was good—incredible, in fact—but I need to be on my way now. You see, I'm from—"

"Enough," he growls in a tone that makes every single coherent thought vanish from my head. "You are one of the lost Omegas, and I have found you. Ulf has seen fit to bring me this most wonderful gift. It would be an insult to him not to keep you."

I swallow, trying to moisten my parched throat and corral my thoughts back into some semblance of order. But I'm exhausted, and the way he smells, the ease with which he's holding me, the heat of his smooth magenta skin are all making it impossible to focus. "I'm not a gift," I mumble, wishing I had the strength to regain some of my earlier outrage at my predicament. "I'm a person. A human being. Not some inanimate object—or even a pet."

He lifts a single eyebrow. "Pet?" Oddly, the word sounds just like it does in English.

"Yeah… an animal—usually domesticated—that you keep at home. For companionship. People sometimes give them as gifts, although they should only do that when the recipient wants one and has the means and time to devote to it. To look after it properly." Am I giving a demon a lecture on animal welfare right now? While his cum is still oozing out of me in thick rivulets? A sudden flush of shame makes my face hot but I can't tear my eyes away from his intense gaze.

His lips curve in a delighted grin, revealing an unexpected dimple in his left cheek. "I want you," he says. "Pet. Like Plutus. I'll look after you."

I'm about to protest again, to demand that he puts me down and releases me, but then I weigh my options. It's highly unlikely that he would let me go without a fight. And if he did? What then? Where would I go? Alkarvi and his acolytes would drag me back to him, or maybe decide to offer me up to some other monster to appease Ulf or some other higher power. So I'd wander around aimlessly on this alien planet, butt naked from the waist down, vulnerable to heck knows what kinds of danger, liable to get killed and eaten, or starve to death if I don't manage to find someone who will help me…

Or… I could go with the demon currently holding me. Of course, I barely know him, but surely if he was going to kill and eat me, he'd have done that already? Another wave of his delicious scent floods my senses and makes my clit tingle. If I go with him, I could get something to drink, maybe some food, a bath…

And if I'm completely honest with myself, it wouldn't be

the worst thing in the world if he wanted to fuck me again. Just the thought makes me shudder with longing.

"Renee," he rasps in that dark, gravelly voice. "Mine." He clutches me to his strong chest and his wings unfurl with a powerful snap. His body tenses and, with a leap and a great whooshing sound that blows my hair off my face, we're airborne. My belly lurches as we ascend.

The black and barren land falls away. Up here, the air is deliciously cool. We're gliding over the lake of fire, over patches of the lava that have dried to a dark crust, and the angry orange seams that roil and surge.

I should be terrified but I feel weirdly secure in his arms, even when a single slip-up on his part would mean my instant death. With no other option, I press my face against his scalding chest and close my eyes, forcing myself to *accept what I cannot change*, as my therapist used to say.

The demon is taking me home.

At least things can't get any weirder.

THREE

Krav

FOR THE FIRST time since I can remember, I am experiencing something I never have before—something I never thought I would. I'm in rut.

Ulf only knows how the Stone King managed it, but he wrought a miracle: there is a living, breathing, female Omega in my arms.

And she is a beauty.

I didn't believe my *jynx* was telling the truth until I was almost upon her. Until her scent hit me and I lost control. I never intended to take her right there, up against the *cex* tree, but I couldn't stop myself.

Another brand new experience. I pride myself on my self-control.

But her wild mane of hair—red blended with glinting gold, like a Pyredii fire-stone—her translucent skin, her bare, round thighs and generous, heaving breasts combined with the most heady aroma of *leeberries*, *talliox* flowers, and musk to make my senses reel. In that moment, I had to fuck her. Nothing else mattered.

It was the quickest, clumsiest coupling of my life but also easily the best.

So far.

Now I am taking her home, where I will seduce her properly. Show her how I prefer to pleasure a female. And how she can pleasure me.

Ulf, but her cunt felt good fluttering around my cock. Just the memory is enough to make me hard again.

I clutch her tighter to my chest as we approach my castle. Luckily for her, she did not resist coming with me beyond that single feeble protest. I would not have enjoyed forcibly bending her to my will so soon after meeting, but I would have done it.

Once we are back in my quarters, I snatch up a cloak and cast a longing glance at my bed before taking her past it, through to the dining hall. Ulf only knows how long she was tied to the tree. She must be incredibly thirsty, and probably hungry as well. My new Omega, my pet, will need plenty of stamina for all the things I intend to do to her.

I set her gently on her feet and wrap her in my cloak, keeping a possessive hand on her arm as she looks around.

"Welcome to my home, Renee," I say. "I've had refreshments prepared for you."

"Thank god. I'm so thirsty."

I steer her to the neatly set table, easing her into a chair. The furniture dwarfs her small frame, but she doesn't seem to notice. She picks up the nearest goblet and sniffs it cautiously.

"What's this?" she asks.

"*Hima* juice."

"Is it safe for humans?"

"Oh yes." My servants will have done their research. "It's very refreshing."

She scrunches up her cute little nose. "Will it get me drunk?"

I chuckle. "No. Although I do have something stronger, if you'd like it."

"No, this is fine." Raising the goblet to her delectable mouth, she takes a small sip, and hums. Her pink tongue flicks over her lips, and my groin tightens. She drinks greedily, draining the whole cup in one go. "That's real nice! Is there any more?"

She licks her lips again and I dig my talons into my palm. I want to grab the jug and toss it across the room, then fuck her right on the table. My tail flicks behind me.

"Of course." I motion for her to sit down, and she does. "Help yourself." I point to the jug and take the seat beside her. "Are you hungry?"

"I am."

"Then eat." I put a little of everything on her plate. "Tell me what you like—and what you don't." I don't usually care so much for another's comfort but something in me aches to please her.

She picks up a *leeberry* tart and nibbles it gingerly while I fill my own plate. Renee is not the only one who will need stamina for what I have planned.

"How do you like that, my little pet?" I ask after a short while.

"These are real good," she says, indicating the tarts before pointing to the *javix*. "Not so keen on that. Honestly, though, I was so hungry I would have eaten anything." She pauses and glances at the floor, suddenly bashful. "I... er... do you have a bathroom here? Facilities?"

Ulfdammit. Considering how similar our physiologies seem to be, I should have anticipated this need. "Certainly. Just through that door." I point, debating whether to go with her but deciding against it. There are no windows in that room, no means of escape.

"Thanks. I'll be right back."

I watch her go, cursing myself for wrapping her in that

heavy cloak which now hides her irresistible body. Her curves should always be on display for me. While I wait for her return, I make mental notes of the outfits I will create for her, and my cock grows impossibly hard.

The dining room windows give an impressive view of Mount Vracor. It's stopped smoking, even though it was rumbling earlier, threatening to erupt.

Interesting. Something cooled its inner turmoil. If the volcano did track my moods, it would be scalding and turgid, vibrating with tension and ready to spew. Like my cock.

After an interminable wait, my pet still hasn't returned and my patience is at an end. I stalk over to the bathing room door and yank it open.

A cloud of steam hits me in the face.

My Omega is in the shower, the hot water sluicing in rivulets over her naked, gleaming body. Opening her eyes, she spots me and gives a startled yelp.

"Sorry," she stammers, "I know I should've asked but I was just so dusty—"

Before she's finished her sentence, I have shucked off my clothing and joined her, my wings quivering, my heart pounding with the need to take her again. "Bad pet," I scold, wrapping a hand lightly around her throat and bending down to speak directly into her ear. "I should spank you."

I expect her to react with horror to my threat but instead her pulse speeds up beneath my fingertips and when she raises her big green eyes to meet mine, the desire in them is unmistakable.

"Oho, what have we here? Could it be that the thought of being disciplined excites my new Omega?"

She lets out a whimper which goes straight to my groin. I slide my free hand between her bare thighs, cupping her slick cunt. Her clit is rigid against my palm.

"It's nothing to be ashamed of," I croon. "You wouldn't be the first female to enjoy being dominated. Controlled.

Rewarded when she behaves…" I grind my palm harder against her clit and she clutches my shoulders with a gasp, "or punished when she's bad." Without waiting for a response, I flip her around and bend her over my hip, slapping her plump ass three times, hard, enjoying the way my handprint appears immediately, scarlet on her pale skin.

Renee cries out but when I slide my finger between her legs once again, still holding her bent at the waist, she's dripping.

"So much slick," I say, "so much wetter than before. Your thighs are trembling and your little clit is pulsing so hard I can feel it. Do you need release, sweet thing?"

Her answering groan is raw and helpless.

"Ask me. No, *beg* me for it. Beg me to let you come."

Renee whimpers but doesn't speak. The conflict raging inside her is palpable and I'm relishing it.

"Now, pet, or I will have to spank you some more." I wait a beat. Two. Three. More slick drips into my palm. "Very well. Don't say I didn't warn you."

Tucking her more firmly under my arm, I use my tail to steady her while I raise my hand and begin, slapping her with careful, measured swats which echo around the room. Renee is gasping, her whole body tense against me, but I don't stop until I've painted her ass, hips and even her thighs a deliciously rosy pink.

My cock is pounding, oozing already, aching to be back inside her tight, slick heat but my desire to dominate everyone and everything has always included my sexual partners, and as a result I find it much more fulfilling to draw things out. To tease. To torture. To toy.

As the echoes of the last ringing slap fade, I grip one plump buttock, squeezing it savagely before sliding my hand back between her thighs. "Ask me," I demand, grazing her slick, swollen sex with the lightest touch, "beg me to make you come. Your clit is twice as big as it was before. You can't hide anything from me."

"Please," Renee croaks at last, and I'm surprised at the rush of pride in my chest. "Please... I need to..."

"Need to... what?" My fingertip is drawing circles around her nubbin now, almost brushing it but not quite.

"Oh god, to *come*, goddamnit! I need to freaking come!"

I chuckle. "We need to work on your begging, sweetheart. I know you're all achy and desperate but ask again... nicely."

There's a pause while she trembles against me and takes a ragged breath. "Please make me come..."

"Good girl! With pleasure." She's so aroused that she climaxes almost the moment my fingertip slides across her clit but I draw it out as much as I can with precise, rhythmic strokes and whispered encouragement. "There we go... come for me, my pet... come nice and hard... let it all out... it's so hot the way your cunt is clenching against my palm... makes me wish I was deep inside you again so you could grip me instead..."

My Omega is whimpering as I pleasure her, every muscle in her body tense as she rides the waves of orgasm, rivers of slick gushing over my hand and down my wrist until, at last, she lets out a final, primal groan and goes limp against me.

Grinning, I remove my soaked hand from her sex and lift it to my lips, desperate to taste her. Her scent explodes on my tongue and I lick my canines as they lengthen.

Renee doesn't resist when I draw her up to face me and once more wrap my fingers possessively around her throat. Her eyes are glazed, her lips slightly parted. She's panting.

"Such a good girl," I praise her. "Did you come nice and hard?"

She nods. Her plump breasts are rising and falling rapidly and I lean down, taking one of her nipples between my teeth, rolling my tongue over it, increasing the pressure of my bite until she cries out and digs her nails into my shoulder.

"Good," I say, straightening and guiding her back under the still-cascading stream of water. "Because now it's *my* turn."

<hr>

I'm in heaven… and a demon brought me here. One touch from the Demon King and a chorus of angels bursts into freaking song. I've never felt anything like it.

Who knew sex could be this good?

When the bathroom door opened and he came prowling through the steam like the devil himself, I damn near passed out—but that terror turned into immediate arousal the moment his scent hit me.

And when he threatened to spank me… Oh. My. God. I've always had a slight suspicion I might be a bit kinky. I devour novels where the heroines are taken in hand, and I've fantasized plenty about being fucked every which way by a big, growly, dominant hero—human or monster—but not even in my wildest dreams did I think it could be *this* good. There's a fever burning in my body, a hunger for this horned monster that only his epic cock can satisfy.

Now I understand why some submissives talk about worshiping their masters. I used to roll my eyes and wonder what kinds of daddy issues a girl must have to want to kneel for a guy, but I get it now. Naked in the shower with the Demon King, nothing else matters but that he keeps touching me. That I please him.

And if he doesn't fuck me now, hard, my insides will collapse and I will die.

One of his huge paws slides around the back of my neck, and I shiver. "Look at me." His voice is a commanding growl I couldn't disobey if I wanted to.

His eyes are like glittering rainbows but his pupils make my breath catch. They're vertical slits, like a snake's. Or a dragon. Or a demon, I guess. Were they like that before? I don't think—

"Now it's your turn to pleasure me," he says, yanking my thoughts back to the present. "Are you going to be a good girl and get on your knees?"

"Yes," I whisper, praying I can get my mouth around him. Even though I just had the most epic orgasm of my life, the gnawing ache in my pussy is back, intensifying with every word he says.

Leaning down, he croons directly into my ear, his breath warming my wet skin. "If you do it well, I might give you a reward." His sudden touch between my legs makes me jump and I gasp when he brushes my clit. His tail strokes my butt. "Would you like that?"

"Yes, Master." The honorific leaves my lips before I even registered I was going to say it. The hell is going on here? Am I under some kind of weird spell that turned me into an insatiable sex slave?

The demon's lips curve into a wicked grin. "*Master.* I like that." For a moment, I think he's going to kiss me, but instead he licks the seam of my mouth before placing his hands on my shoulders and pushing me gently, firmly, to my knees.

This is the first chance I have to take a close look at his dick but before I can blink to focus, he's guiding my head to his groin and rubbing the tip of his enormous cock over my face. I open my mouth obediently, inexplicably hungry to taste him, anticipating his girth but still surprised by just how much I have to stretch my lips around the rigid shaft.

I reach up automatically to stroke the parts I can't suck but his growl stops me dead. "No. Hands behind your back. Keep them there. And spread your knees wider. I want to relish the scent of your slick while I fuck your throat."

As turned on as I am, I'm tempted to argue that there's no

way he'll be doing that. Even if he wasn't as wide as a can of shaving cream, even if gag reflexes didn't exist, the extras on his cock would make throat-fucking impossible. Now I know how he hits my G-spot so damn well. Solid, bumpy ridges run along the top, bottom, and sides of his shaft, rasping over my outstretched tongue.

He tastes as good as he smells—bitterest chocolate with a hint of salt and smoky whiskey—and I wish I could take him deeper. Kneeling before him, naked and wet, my hands clasped obediently behind my back and my thighs spread wide, I lick and suck him greedily, amazed at how turned on I am. Every grunt of pleasure he gives goes straight to my clit.

"Such a good little pet." He's stroking my hair, guiding my movements, pushing a little deeper. My initial panic gives way to disbelief when my throat relaxes like it has a mind of its own until he's halfway in. "Ulf, that feels so—" His words fade into a roaring, primal growl that reverberates through my entire body. My pussy clenches hard, and blazing stars dot the insides of my eyelids. There's a surge of warmth between my legs and I feel like I might pass out.

The next thing I know, my nose is bumping up against his groin and he's fucking my throat with smooth thrusts, pulling almost all the way out of my mouth before plunging back in to the hilt. A tiny faraway voice in my head is asking how the heck this is even possible but I'm too filled with pride and raging lust to care.

My knees are aching, my thighs are trembling with the strain of staying in position, and I'm desperate to come but I'm disappointed when the Demon King yanks his cock out of my mouth. His tail wraps around me, steadying me as he tugs me to my feet.

He's still growling, the animalistic sound making my very core vibrate. His leathery wings are spread, flared about his horns and head, dripping with water. Clamping his hands around my waist, he hoists me into the air with ridiculous ease, lifting me until my pussy's level with his mouth.

I grab his horns and gasp—even they are hot to the touch. I slide my hands down their length and they pulse against my palms. He shudders as if I'd stroked his cock. *His horns are sensitive. Interesting. Guess I'd better not use them to brace myself.*

For a long, agonizing moment, he's still, growling, and I know he's breathing in my scent. If this were any other sexual encounter with any other guy, I'd probably feel some level of shame in being sniffed like an animal but in this weird alternate universe, it turns me on even more.

I dangle helplessly in his hold, his warm breath searing my drenched pussy, trembling with anticipation. At last, he draws me closer and licks into me, his tongue sliding over my clit in the most delicious, heart-stopping way. I come instantly with an inhuman groan, every muscle in my groin clenching so hard, it's borderline painful.

As he did last time with his fingers, the demon draws out my orgasm with eerie precision, somehow knowing the exact rhythm and pressure to use. At the same time, his grip on my waist tightens until it hurts, cutting off my ability to breathe so all I can do is convulse and clench against his tongue.

Only when my final flutters of pleasure have subsided does he relax his grip—but instead of setting me on the ground, he lowers me directly onto his cock, impaling me fully with one smooth stroke.

I can't help but cry out as my pussy burns with the stretch. His tail seeks the small of my back, pushing me until I'm flush against his heated skin.

"You're a naughty little pet." He draws almost all the way out of me, pauses, and slams his cock home. "You came all over my tongue, practically drowning me in your slick," another hard thrust, "but you didn't ask for permission first." Thrust.

"I'm sorry," I croak, my mind spinning with sensation overload, "I couldn't help it. Your tongue—"

He's stopped fucking me but his cock is still inside me, my legs wrapped around his waist. "I don't want to hear your excuses. Do you agree that you should be punished?"

Just that single word is enough to make me shiver. "Yes… no… I don't know. Please…"

"Please what?"

"Please keep fucking me."

"You can beg better than that, sweetheart."

It's almost impossible to think straight but I force myself to focus. "Please keep fucking me, Master."

The words have barely left my mouth before he turns feral. With a growl, he spins us around until my back is wedged up against the cold, smooth wall, and starts to pound me with savage ferocity. I feel like he's splitting me in half—but it hurts so good. Hooking one massive, bronze-swirled forearm under my right knee, he forces that leg further up and out, changing the angle so I'm no longer getting any friction where I need it most. I whimper in frustration.

"This is your punishment, pet," he rasps. "Since you came without permission, you don't get to come again. This is for my pleasure."

"No, please!" His whispered threats only make me more desperate to have what he's denying me, and he knows it, damn him.

"This is what you were made for. What your body was made for. To take my cock, my pain, my seed. You're mine now. I own you."

Every word sends tingles skittering along my sex. My clit is thumping with need.

He's thrusting faster now, pounding me against the wall. I meet his gaze, hoping he'll change his mind when he sees my expression, but his eyes are glazed.

"My… pet… Omega…" The Demon King's roar mingles

with my shout of pleasure-pain as his cock thickens further, stretching me beyond what I should be capable of handling.

My pussy flutters as he fills it with rhythmic jerks, his outstretched wings quivering, his eyes closed, his head thrown back, lost in pleasure. Just when I think he can't still be coming, he lets out one final groan and relaxes against me. He lowers my leg to a more comfortable position and leans in, nuzzling my neck in a gesture completely at odds with the savagery he just displayed.

We stay like that for a few moments, locked together and silent. I breathe him in, trying—and failing—to think straight. His skin is so hot and smooth against mine. The shower is still running but we're nowhere near it, and as the water cools on my naked body, I shiver.

The demon immediately lifts me away from the wall and slides his arms around me. "You're cold. My apologies," he murmurs, shifting me higher so he can slide out of me. I gasp at the sharp pang and close my eyes, embarrassed by the amount of cum gushing all over the floor.

He pets my pussy with his huge paw, rubbing the silky fluid of our combined juices between his talon-tipped fingers. "You please me, sweet one."

I shiver again.

"I will take care of you." He strokes my wet hair from my face as I droop in his arms. His tail snakes around my waist, holding me against him. "You need warmth and comfort. Rest." He carries me under the warm shower spray and holds me up as the water sluices the evidence of our epic sex-fest from my body. After jabbing the lever to turn the shower off, he carries me out of the bathroom. If he's tired of toting me everywhere, he doesn't show it. "The rut... I got carried away."

He lays me on the enormous bed and covers me with several thick, fluffy blankets, tucking them around me as if I were a child. There's that soft, Daddy-dom side of him again.

"That's better," he croons, leaning over me and smoothing a massive hand over the ornate coverlet. "Relax. You'll feel better in a moment." He uses his tail to twitch the rumpled blankets at my feet into place.

I'm so sleepy. Full of questions, but also incredibly tired. A rush of warmth spreads through my chest. The demon is growling again, but it's softer. Soothing. Like a purr. "Why are you doing that?"

He either doesn't hear or is ignoring my question. "Sleep for a while, my pet. You need to regain your strength. There are so many more ways I plan to rut you."

"Is that what you call it here? Rutting?" I yawn. I want to crawl closer to him and lay my ear against his chest so the purr rumbles through me, but my limbs are heavy and my muscles are weak.

He chuckles like I've said something dumb. "What else would you call it when an Alpha takes an Omega? We can fuck Betas but only an Omega will send us into rut."

I barely understood three words out of that entire statement and want so badly for him to clarify but I'm too drowsy to talk. I want him to stretch out on the bed beside me and hold me in his arms, but my lips won't move, so I cover his huge hand with mine. His purr grows louder and I can't fight it anymore. I let my eyelids droop. I'll nap for a bit, and when I wake up, I'll ask him everything I want to know.

Hopefully, I'll get some answers.

FOUR

Krav

I smooth the covers over my sleeping Omega. She's so tiny, dwarfed by my grand bed. Ulf chose her well—she's perfect for me sexually. She took what I gave her, and welcomed it.

I'm reluctant to leave her. I've never wanted to cuddle in bed with a female before. It must be the rut.

I force myself to extricate my hand from her dainty fingers. She may be a gift, but she must learn her place as my pet. It would not do to treat her otherwise. I command the *jynx* to watch over her and alert me the moment she wakes. *Because she is my possession and in my care, and I am a good Master. Not because I need to be near her.*

With one last glance at Renee's sleeping form, I leave the room. The ornate bronze doors close silently behind me. For a moment, I stand in the hall, unsure. Every cell in my body longs to return to her side.

But that's ridiculous. I am a king, with better things to do than watch over a sleeping female.

I will check on my other pet, Plutus. No matter that every step I take away from Renee feels wrong.

Outside, the air is clearer than it has been in a long time. Mount Vracor is quiet. Has the volcano ceased stirring because Ulf sent me an Omega? Impossible.

It is said that Omegas soothe their Alphas, but I feel the opposite of calm. My tail twitches and my wings ache with the need to unfurl. As if I should fly back to Renee's side.

I ignore all of it.

My beloved *styxian* is delighted to see me as always, ruffling his wings and snorting flashes of violet flame through his nostrils.

"We have a new companion," I tell him, reaching up to scratch the top of his feathered head. "Would you believe a real Omega just appeared in my kingdom?"

Plutus is incapable of speech, of course, but we understand each other nonetheless. Talking to him sometimes helps me sort out my thoughts.

"I look forward to introducing you both." I chuckle. "Now I have two pets."

Plutus shakes himself, spreading his wings and cocking his head. His golden eyes are alert, watchful. Like me, he is a predator.

"You might be wondering why I called her a pet," I say, opening the nearby chest of his snacks and selecting a *crius*. Even though they're tough, scaly little creatures, Plutus adores them. There's no accounting for taste. "But truthfully, I have no need of a queen. No desire for heirs. Offspring cause nothing but trouble. Especially demon offspring." Ulf knows, my father felt the same way.

I toss Plutus his treat, and the *styxian* catches it neatly with his beak. Their reflexes are like lightning.

"Nevertheless, I will keep her. She belongs to me." I allow myself a fantasy: Renee chained at my feet, wearing nothing but a collar and leash. Not only is she submissive, as all Omegas—all females, in fact—should be, she's also stunningly beautiful. "She is perfect, and rutting her is exquisite. Her body was made for pleasure. My pleasure."

Plutus bobs his head, his intent gaze darting to the chest and back to me.

"So greedy," I chide even as I go to get more treats and fling them at him, one by one. "Just like your master." Except my vast appetite happens to be sexual rather than for food. I can still hardly believe my luck. Putting on a disguise and venturing out to brothels to find pleasure slaves is a tiresome process, which is why I only chose that route when my lust was too great and I could no longer stand it. Now I have my Omega, I will never have to bother with that nonsense again. Thank Ulf.

As I bend to close the chest, Plutus rears up and lets out an ear-splitting shriek, shaking his huge wings.

"I can't take you out today," I say. "I must remain to care for my Omega when she wakes up. Would you like to go alone?" Unlocking the cage door, I tug it open and stand beside it, gesturing to indicate that he's free to go. He always returns. We have a bond of sorts.

Plutus cocks his head for a moment as if considering it.

"Last chance," I tell him. "Otherwise you'll have to wait until tomorrow."

With a snort, the magnificent creature barrels past me, streaking across the ground and taking flight, his striking turquoise and gold feathers glinting in the fading sunlight.

"Have fun," I call after him, tugging the cage door back into place. My shadow servants will inform me of his return.

I long to hurry back to the Omega, but force myself to maintain a sedate pace through the castle. Here and there, I pause, checking things are in order. My *jynx* are efficient, rushing to obey my every command. They are created from pure magic, and know my will.

The room they're preparing for my new pet is close to my own suite of chambers. I want easy access to her at all times, but my solitude is also important to me. This arrangement gives us the best of both worlds. My parents took it even further, choosing to reside on separate wings *and* levels of the castle. So great was their mutual loathing that I often wondered how they managed to have me. Unsurprisingly, I was their only child.

While I know some couples choose to mesh their lives in every way, eating, sleeping and even working with one another, I find the notion abhorrent. After all, I'm a demon, and demons prefer to keep to themselves. We are the most powerful of Ulf's creations, formed from the fires of Mount Vracor to rule this hellscape. As superior beings, we do not crave the companionship of others. Only the weak get lonely.

I reach my bedchamber and admire the still sleeping form of my new plaything. Huddled under the coverlet, her spectacular curves are hidden from view, but her mane of crimson hair spills over my pillows. Instead of Ulfarri markings, tiny orange dots adorn her skin, especially the bridge of her nose. Her lips are slightly parted and I can barely resist the urge to lick them.

As if she can feel my gaze on her, she stirs and rolls over. I hesitate, wondering whether to wake her. Her scent lights a fire in my loins. My tail swishes behind me. I should have taken this chance to get some sleep as well but I'm too on edge. The rut is all-consuming.

Khan, the Wanderer King, exhibited fierce, possessive behavior when he found the first Omega, the one he made his queen. He clutched her to his chest like his most prized possession, snarling at anyone who dared to glance their way. He even ensured she was drenched in his seed before taking her to the council meeting. At the time, I thought he was overreacting, but now, looking down at the tiny Omega beneath my sheets, I can't say I wouldn't do the same.

Alphas don't like to share.

I pace around the bed, wanting to crawl into it and hold my

pet, but unwilling to disturb her sleep. Both instincts are new to me. I've never wanted prolonged contact with anyone before, including the Beta courtesans I used to visit. Nor would I have thought twice about waking one of them to serve my needs.

Renee is my Omega. She belongs to me. She needs her sleep so she can be strong enough to withstand my sexual demands. My desperate urge to hold her must be a symptom of the rut.

She stirs again, opening her eyes and blinking to focus. I command the orbs to glow brighter, and she flinches when she sees me. "Oh," she says. "So it wasn't a dream."

I sit down on the edge of the bed and reach out to stroke her cheek. "No, pet. Not a dream."

"I… er… I need the bathroom," she says, a delightful flush creeping over her cheeks. It reminds me of the way her skin turns pink when she's aroused, and my cock stiffens.

"You know where it is. Will you be taking another shower?" I raise an eyebrow.

"No. I'll… er… be right back." She makes to get out of bed but stops, her arms folded over the blanket covering her ample chest. "Um… Your Evilness?"

I chuckle inwardly at the common folk's title for me. "You may call me Krav," I say on impulse, curious to hear my name on her lips.

"Krav," she murmurs, and a bolt of lust shoots through me. "I'm naked."

"That you are, sweet one." Her hair has dried and curtains her slender shoulders. The flush spreads over her chest, above her crossed arms.

"Um." Her eyes dart around my bedchamber.

"Suddenly shy? Don't forget I've seen every single inch of your delicious body."

The pink stain on her face deepens. "Well, yeah, but that's different. We were… busy."

"Renee." I use her name intentionally, lowering my voice in a way she can't help but respond to. "You are beautiful in every way. Especially naked. I intend to have you in that state as much as possible, so you may as well get used to it."

She chews her lip and looks down at the blankets still covering her. "Thank you. That's a lovely thing to say, but I'm still... I mean, I'm no teenager anymore. I have stretch marks, scars, the girls aren't what they used to—"

"Enough!" I snarl, gratified when her gaze snaps back to meet mine. Her startled green eyes look almost blue in the soft glow cast by the orbs. "Nobody is permitted to disparage anything that belongs to me. Including you. Do not let me hear you speak that way about yourself again."

There's a pause while a myriad of expressions flit across her face. Then, "Sorry. It's a habit, I guess." Glancing down at her hands, she takes a deep breath. "I think there's some kind of misunderstanding, though."

I raise an eyebrow. "Is that so?"

"Yeah. But... we'll have to discuss it when I get back. Please excuse me for a moment."

"Certainly." I watch as she scrambles out from beneath the covers, admiring the way her ass moves as she hurries in the direction of the bathroom. My handprints have faded from her skin, and I long to mark her again.

But there's no hurry. She's mine now, to use however I please. Forever.

***

Renee

The Demon King—Krav—is so intense. Whenever he fixes me with that mystic topaz gaze, I feel exposed. Vulnerable. Like my soul has been laid bare. And the way he pivots between tenderness and almost callous dominance makes my belly clench.

I'm not usually bothered about being naked—when I'm home alone, anyway—but he devours me with his eyes and makes me feel like he's peering through my skin. A couple times now, I've wondered if he can read my thoughts.

I freaking hope not.

Once I'm done in the bathroom, I scuttle back to the bed, tugging the blanket around myself like a shield. Krav hasn't moved; his giant, hulking form is still perched on the edge of the mattress.

Now I'm not asleep or coming my brains out, I take a moment to check him out properly. He's just as imposing as he first seemed when he flew towards me, looming out of the sky like a...

Well. Like a demon.

"You were saying?" His rasping voice breaks into my thoughts. "About a misunderstanding?"

I take a steadying breath, staring down at my hands. "Yeah. So." I'm trying to find the right words. "You seem to be under the impression I *belong* to you." Even saying it aloud sounds ridiculous. "I just wanted to clarify that I don't. I know the... villagers... people... your subjects back there kinda *gave* me to you, but you see, I'm not anyone's *possession.* I'm a free, independent human being."

When I'm brave enough to glance at his face, I'm taken aback by how bemused he looks. At least he's not mad. "You're an Omega," he says at length. "*My* Omega."

"I don't even know what that is!" The sense of unreality I've had since I first opened my eyes yesterday or whenever it was is beginning to fade, and it's slowly hitting me that I *am* on another planet. For real. And I'm talking to an honest-to-god demon monster who has fucked my brains out. Twice.

Krav gives the sigh of a teacher who has to explain something for the millionth time, and shifts to a more comfortable position. "Ulfarri society has three designations," he begins. "Alpha. Beta. Omega."

"Like the Greek alphabet." It helps me to remember things if I use context.

"Do not interrupt," he says grandly and I only just stop myself from rolling my eyes. "Alphas are the strength of society. The warriors. The protectors. The kings."

"Like you," I observe. His answering glare shuts me right back up.

"Betas make up the majority of society. The common folk. The thinkers, artists, manufacturers. And the Omegas are the mothers. The nurturers. The jewels." Reaching out, he caresses my foot through the blanket, and I shiver with renewed longing. Why does his touch make me melt? I shift my leg slightly, determined not to get distracted by desire this time.

"Who decides what you are? Is there a sorting hat of some kind?"

"It is how you are made. Your nature."

"How d'you mean?"

"Alpha/Omega couples always produce Alpha or Omega offspring. Beta couples will usually have Beta children, although on average, around one in five are Alphas." He waves a dismissive hand. "It is said that occasionally, Beta couples have been known to produce Omegas, but it's rare enough to be of no consequence."

"Right. I see. What about Alpha/Beta couples?"

He scoffs, like I just said something ridiculous. "Those couplings never result in offspring. They're biologically incompatible."

I blink, trying to absorb all this stuff. "So why do you keep saying I'm an Omega? I'm not from here. I'm a human. From Earth."

"Yes, yes. Like the others." His hand creeps up my leg and curls around my thigh but that last statement has me reeling.

"What others?" My voice sounds like it's coming from somewhere far away.

"The other Hoo-man Omegas," he says. His touch on my thigh tickles, and my leg jerks. He wraps his tail around my ankle to keep me still. "Some of the other kings wanted queens to give them heirs, and since Alphas can only breed with Omegas—and there are none to be found here—they devised a way to bring some over from your planet."

"But we don't have Omegas on Earth!" I bleat. His so-called explanations are only leading to more questions.

"No, but your biology makes it possible for you to be turned into one. As the other queens were. As *you* were." His tone has thickened. His hand is creeping towards my groin and my body responds with a surge of liquid heat. His scent is getting stronger.

"I doubt it. Surely I'd remember that." I squeeze my thighs together to halt his wandering hand, struggling to focus on our conversation. "And even if I was… turned into one… that still wouldn't make me your property!"

Krav lets out a low, warning growl and pounces, forcing me onto my back, caging me within his hulking arms. My heart flutters like a trapped bird, but heat surges in my core.

His face is just inches from mine, his breath warm on my lips. My skin tingles. "You are mine." His tone brooks no argument. I whimper as he bends down and nuzzles the spot where my neck meets my shoulder, inhaling deeply. "You smell like an Omega." He presses his lower body against mine and my thighs part automatically. He grinds against me and I can feel the ridges of his cock massaging my clit even through the blankets. Pleasure darts through me and I let out a helpless moan. "You react like an Omega," he continues, grinding faster until I'm on the edge.

"Oh fuck, please," I beg, humiliated by how easily he can turn me on. "Krav—"

"You even choose to call me *Master*," he rasps, shifting so he's no longer pressed up against me.

My entire focus has narrowed to that throbbing, thumping, desperate spot between my thighs. "I… I…" I'm so aroused, I've lost the ability to speak.

"Say it," he growls, and I groan as my pussy reacts with another gush of *slick*, as he calls it.

"I…" I want to obey but my tongue is refusing to form words.

With a snarl, he rears up and yanks the blankets off my naked body, flinging them aside. My nipples tighten in the cool air. He grips one, squeezing hard enough to make me yelp before his hand slides lower, down over my belly and between my legs. "Who owns you?"

His fingertips are grazing the outer edges of my labia and dipping in and out, sending sparks of need through me. I can do nothing but whimper.

He leans down to whisper directly in my ear. His tone has changed. He's crooning. "Just say it, pet. One little sentence and I will make you come so, so hard…"

His slippery fingertip finds my clit and circles it. I buck and writhe, trying to get the right friction.

"What's the matter, sweetheart? Have you lost your tongue?" He chuckles darkly. "Do you need mine? Right here?" His fingertip moves agonizingly lower, slipping deep inside me. I cry out. "You have two choices. You can tell me what I want to hear, and I will tongue-fuck your tight, slick hole and hard, swollen little clit until you see stars…"

I clench around him. He tugs his finger out and slaps me right there, his huge hand landing squarely between my thighs. The sharp pain fades instantly, only amplifying my need.

"Or," he continues conversationally, "we can keep doing this. Getting you so, so close—" He's stroking my clit again and my entire body tenses, on the precipice… but at the first flutter of orgasm, he lifts his hand away, "—and denying you, over and over again."

My frustration erupts out of me in a howl as I buck, seeking his touch.

"Poor little needy Omega," he croons. "Want me to help you?"

I nod, gasping.

He slaps my aching, throbbing pussy again, his palm landing hard on my clit, and I shriek. "Oh dear, was that not what you meant?" I can hear the smile in his voice.

"No!"

"You see? You *can* speak. Use your words." He's using his palm to rub the sting from my sensitive sex. Tendrils of pleasure curl through my core.

"Please…" His touch is driving me higher, higher… I close my eyes.

"You know what I want from you."

The bitter chocolate whisky scent fills my nostrils, and I groan. I'm so damn close. My toes start to tingle.

"*You own me, Master,*" Krav whispers harshly, his fingertip once again finding my most sensitive spot and rubbing back and forth. "Say it."

I don't want to admit it, but I'm loving the power exchange. I might fight the desire, the need to surrender, but I can't deny my body's responses. The way Krav dominates me is the hottest thing ever. I just can't form a coherent sentence—not with the way he's touching me.

The orgasm building in me now threatens to be the biggest one yet. I suck in a ragged breath, clenching my pussy in preparation. I'm almost there. One more second of this, and—

He removes his hand, chuckling at my howl of frustration. "I could do this all night, pet."

The words, when they finally spill out of me, are a

desperate, rushed, breathless plea. "YouownmeMaster! You do! Please! For the love of everything holy, *please!*"

He's licking me before I've even finished the sentence. His lips envelop my entire sex and he sucks it hungrily, lapping at my labia and clit before making good on his promise to tongue-fuck me. I'm adrift, unmoored, swept away on a raging sea of bliss. I reach for him to steady myself, and my hands find his horns. They're smooth and hard beneath my fingertips, the bases of them pulsing with heat. The feel of them only turns me on more.

How long is his dang tongue, anyhow? He's tormenting me with slow, deep thrusts, his top lip resting just above the straining bud I want him so desperately to stimulate.

I rock my hips but he just moves with me. When he chuckles, it reverberates through my very soul.

"Oh goddamnit, *please…*" I no longer care that I'm begging. I'll tell him anything he wants to hear—that down is up, and I'm the queen of Sheba—if it means I'll get off.

His hands clamp down on my hips, and that reminder of his crazy strength shocks me into stillness. Pinpricks of pain stab my skin and I glance down to see his claws digging into my flesh. Not hard enough to draw blood, but enough to make my belly flip with a combination of fear and lust.

He's still driving his tongue inexorably in and out of me and all I can do is lie there, whimpering. It feels so amazingly good but I can't come unless he goes back to my clit.

After what feels like a hundred years, he raises his head and fixes me with that intense rainbow gaze. "Still want release?"

I bite back a huff of impatience. "Yes. Please."

"Ask. You will always ask permission from now on."

"Seriously?" Fire flashes in his eyes and his claws tighten just the tiniest bit on my bare hips. "Okay, okay!"

"And you'd better remain completely still. I'm sure you don't want me to scratch you."

"Krav—*Master*," I correct myself when his brows lower, "I don't think I can—"

He cuts off my protest with a long, languorous lick from my entrance to my clit and back down. "You will try, sweetheart. For me." His tongue finds that spot again and I'm back on the brink in seconds.

"Oh Master, please… may I… come?"

"Now," he growls against my wet flesh and the orgasm engulfs me, my pussy contracting so violently, it takes my breath away. The first spasm makes me want to buck and writhe but the sharp scratch of his deadly claws on my hips forces me to stay still. I don't know why that amplifies everything, but it does. Unable to move, I howl instead, sobbing my way through the tidal wave of release until I'm hoarse. Drained. Spent.

Even though I'm done, his tongue doesn't stop curling around my clit, and now it's too intense. Without thinking, I try to wriggle away—until his sharp talons rake my hips, reminding me that he's in complete control, and I'm not going anywhere until he decides I can.

Why does that drive me so damn wild? His tongue moves further south, stabbing my pussy, and I groan at how good it feels. He licks lower still, lapping at my most private hole. I toss my head, shame making my cheeks burn. "No, please… don't… not there."

He looks up at me. "You don't like it?"

"I… er… I've never done it before. Been licked there, I mean. But it feels…" I cast about for the right word and come up empty.

"I own you, pet," he says, "all of you. If I wish to lick you here, I will."

"Just licking?" There's no way I could take his enormous cock back there. Not even if I wanted to. And I don't want to…

He must sense my sudden fear and is quick to reassure

me. "Just licking." The unspoken *for now* hangs in the air for a moment before he bends down and slides his tongue over my ass.

I knew rimming was a thing people did but truthfully, I never saw the point in it—until now. This feels like heaven on a plate when Krav's the one doing it to me. I'm moaning again, the knowledge that I can't move, that all I can do is lie there and take it only serving to increase the pleasure.

He licks up and down every square inch of flesh between my legs until I'm coiled like a spring, trembling, aching for him. And when he rears up and fits the head of his cock at my pussy, I open my eyes to find him gazing down at me. His pupils are slits again, his lips set in a firm line. The bronze-swirled muscles of his violet chest ripple with his movement as he hooks my legs up over his shoulders and drives into me slowly… stretching… invading…

My pussy is still sore from our last round and I gasp as he forces me open, filling me beyond what I thought possible, the crests along his shaft hitting places inside me I didn't know I had.

His growl erupts from his throat and my body reacts like it always does—with a shudder of pleasure and a gush of slick.

Leaning forward, his eyes still fixed on mine, Krav uses my wrists to pin me down. The different angle is putting friction on my clit, and I gasp as sparks shoot through my core.

"I own you," he rasps as he begins to thrust hard. "You're my pet. Mine."

I can only nod, too swept away by the sensations of him fucking me to speak.

"Keep your eyes on me," he says, thrusting harder.

It hurts so damn good. Who knew pain could amplify pleasure this way? Another orgasm is building… I'm getting closer with each thrust, each crushing press of my clit.

His tail is busy, too, snaking around him to tickle my rear. Press between my ass cheeks. Circle the sensitive rosette of skin and probe lightly, testing. The sensation makes my pussy gush. I'm close—

As if he can read my mind, Krav warns me, "Don't forget to ask."

He's getting thicker inside me, I'm sure of it. My entire core pulses around him as if drawing him deeper. As if that were possible.

"I love to feel you stretched wide around my cock," Krav whispers. "You fit me perfectly. Like you were made for me. Made for my pleasure. For me to fill you. And when you climax, that little cunt snatching around me, Ulf…" His groan almost pushes me over the edge.

"Please, Master, I need to come…"

"Wait… with me… now…"

He spreads his huge black wings, throws his head back, and roars. With every beat of his wings, his body rocks against mine, pushing his pulsing cock deeper. His cum boils out of him, searing me, and the combination of terror and lust sends me soaring over the edge.

I writhe and shudder beneath the magnificent monster, ecstasy lighting up my every nerve ending. All my thoughts white out except for one:

I won't be satisfied by anyone else ever again.

FIVE

Renee

Is this my life now? Sex slave to a freaking *demon*?

I mean, sure, he can do magic, gives me anything I want, and has awakened a whole new kinky side of me, but…

I shift into *downward dog*, trying to concentrate on my breathing. Yoga always used to let me escape my tumbling thoughts, all the busy chatter that constantly scurries through my brain. Not today. No matter how many times I drag my focus back to my breath, I can't stop ruminating over my situation—more specifically, how I feel about said situation.

When I first went with Krav, I had hoped that I would get answers to my many, many questions.

Unfortunately, I'm still waiting. Apart from telling me all that confusing Greek alphabet stuff, the demon has been infuriatingly tight-lipped. Any time I mention the other human Omegas, or ask how I got turned into one and brought to a different planet, he brushes me off—usually distracting me with a growl, which turns my insides into mush. He's fucked me so much over the past little while that I had to beg him for a breather, which is why I'm now in my room, on the teal yoga mat he made for me, trying to quiet my mind.

I go into a brief plank, then move into *cobra*, grateful I can remember the poses, at least. So much of my memory is missing, and it's infuriating.

Krav was curious and surprisingly indulgent when I asked him for a mat. I had to explain what yoga was—which was no mean feat, let me tell you—and then detail the characteristics of a good mat. To my astonishment, he listened carefully for a moment and then, with a swirl of silver sparks, conjured one up out of thin air.

The guy can literally do magic. He went on to explain that that's how I'm able to take him all the way in my throat and pussy—with a little enchanted help.

"I would break you, otherwise," he told me.

No kidding. But when I asked him whether my other reactions were also induced by some kind of spell, he denied it. Which means—assuming he was being truthful—that I enjoy pain with my pleasure. That I have a submissive streak that makes me want to kneel at his big feet and worship at the altar of his raw dominance.

I've always been curious about BDSM, and now I'm getting the chance to explore it, it's better than I ever imagined. But I'd better stop thinking about that, otherwise I'll just get horny again. I heard that some women get a crazy high sex drive when they hit their forties, but this is a whole other level. Being easily aroused and wanting to bang more is one thing. Turning into a demon's slavishly devoted fuckpet is quite another. I wonder if it has something to do with that whole Omega business, and freaking *wish* I could meet and talk to some of the other humans who are here on Ulfaria. Or, hell, just one of them.

Where are they? How did they get here? Are they actively looking for a way to get home? Do their partners treat them well? Do their partners make their clothing, too? Right now, I'm in Krav's idea of *something comfortable*—a green shirt which is basically transparent, and black harem pants. At least I can move in it.

Goddamn that stupid purple asshole for keeping me in the dark about everything. There isn't anyone else here I can ask. Krav lives alone except for a pet I've never seen, and his creepy shadow servants, who flit about silently and do all the menial stuff like housekeeping.

Sliding into *extended child's pose*, I inhale slowly and close my eyes, trying not to think about how much I'd love a latte right about now. Then I'd head over to Texas Roadhouse for some of their delicious starter rolls with that sweet whipped butter…

Mindfulness, I remind myself sternly. *Gratitude. Sure, this is a weird situation but it could be so much worse. You could have died. Krav could have literally killed and eaten you... or not been quite so strikingly attractive... or so focused on your pleasure. Yes, the food is strange, but at least you can eat it, and some of it is even tasty. You can understand what the aliens are saying—and speak their language. You can still do yoga.*

I should just try to take things one day at a time, and be grateful for the silver linings in the meantime.

With fresh resolve, I rise up off my mat and take stock of the room Krav had prepared for me. It's so freaking *bare*. It needs pictures, pillows, rugs, throws, scented candles…

It needs to be welcoming. Right now, there's just a big bed with a metal frame that looms high above it and makes it look like a cage, a bare floor, and a window with what a realtor might call: *a picturesque view of the surrounding lava lake.*

Spinning on my heels, I set off in search of the demon.

Krav is in his library, peering intently at a set of scrolls. When I enter, he looks over and the corner of his mouth quirks up, revealing his dimple. "Pet. What can I do for you?"

"My bedroom. I need… things to make it nice. To make it pretty."

His mystic topaz eyes flash with interest. "Is that so? Do you know why you want these things?"

"Is it important?" As it happens, I have no idea where this sudden urge has come from.

"No. I am happy to give you anything your heart desires."

Aside from answers, I think savagely, but I favor him with a smile. Better to bring him around slowly. Wear him down over time. Cooperate. He doesn't react well when I stamp my feet and demand things. "Thank you." Then, when he makes no move to get up, "Er… d'you think we could do it right now, please?"

"This very moment?"

"Yeah. If that's possible. Please."

Setting his reading aside, he lumbers up out of his chair and I tense as he prowls in my direction, bracing myself for his scent to hit me. The bitter, musky chocolate rolls up through my core and I clench my thighs around the sudden longing. Like he can read my thoughts, Krav shoots me a wink as he strolls past me. "We could do other things in your bedroom, if you prefer."

"I'm okay, thanks." I can't say I'm not tempted, but weirdly, the urge to spruce up my room is stronger than the pulsing in my clit. Besides, I do need to give my nether regions a break. We've done nothing but fuck, eat, and sleep since I arrived.

I follow Krav as he prowls along the corridors of his vast castle. A *jynx* whooshes by in a blur of shadow, making me jump. Will I ever get used to those creepy things? Krav says they're harmless but they startle the crap out of me.

"Here we are," he announces, rather unnecessarily, when we cross the threshold to my room. "Tell me what you need."

"What do you have?" I counter. "Is there a storage closet somewhere?"

He lifts his huge, talon-tipped hands, as big as bear paws. "Tell me what you need, my pet, and I will make it for you."

I say the first thing that comes to mind. "A big, purple pillow with tassels."

His hands move so fast they're a blur and then, a shower of silver sparks later, he hands me a gorgeous cushion.

"Holy fuck. That is a serious talent."

He gives a shrug, his tail flicking out behind him. "You already knew I could do this." I follow his gaze to my yoga mat, which I left spread out on the floor.

"Yeah, but it's still taking some getting used to. Can you make *anything*?"

"Not people. Nothing that can be ingested, like food or drink. And I need to be able to see what I'm making in my mind before my hands can follow."

"So if you can't imagine it, you can't make it?"

He gives a little huff of impatience. "What else do you need for your nest, little Omega?"

"Nest? Weird choice of word. I just want to make my room pretty."

"Because you're nesting."

I open my mouth to argue, then consider his statement. I've been sleeping in this room for a few days already, and this urge to redecorate came out of the blue. "Is that something Omegas do?"

"Yes."

"Why?"

"From what I understand, it's a natural part of the estrus cycle for most."

"Estrus?"

"The period of time when the Omega is most fertile."

His words take a moment to sink in. Krav is a different freaking *species*. The thought that he could put a bun in my oven never entered my head. Until now. "You're saying I'm having this urge to nest because I'm in estrus… in my fertile phase?" I clarify.

"Of course."

My heart is crashing against my ribs. "So… you could get me pregnant?"

His entire expression changes—like he's appalled by the idea—before he quickly schools his features back into neutral. "It's possible."

I blow out a breath, like I've been socked in the gut. I'd always planned to have kids, but when I woke up on my fortieth with a failed marriage behind me and no good potential baby-daddy candidates on the horizon, I had to face facts: it might be too late. But now…

No. I won't think about this now. I'm on a new planet, with a new monster lover, and weird changes in my biology to deal with. I'll mull it over later, in peace. Once I've fixed up this space.

Krav waves an impatient hand. "Is your new room complete with just one cushion?"

"No, of course not. Er… I need sheets. Cotton. Can you make them rose gold?" I love rose gold. At his confused look, I clarify. "Gold but with a pink hue."

"I can try."

I watch him work, touched by his earnest determination to give me exactly what I'm asking for. Soon, he hands me a set of gorgeous sheets, and I stroke the soft fabric with a sigh. "Perfect. Thank you."

His eyes light up at the praise. "What else?"

I list more items and he makes them, one by one, with infinite patience. So different compared with my ex, who used to get so grouchy when I asked him to do things around the house.

We've settled into a comfortable rhythm, and the room is taking shape. In a whirlwind of silver sparks, Krav conjures up a thick, fluffy rug that covers most of the floor between the door and the bed. It transforms the whole space, making it look soft and cozy. The tense muscles in my back unclench.

Krav turns his impressive powers to making me some curtains while I arrange some gorgeous flowers in a vase on my new dressing table. Since he couldn't picture any Earth blooms, I asked him for some pretty Ulfarri alternatives, and the bouquet I'm now fiddling with is just stunning. They're moonflowers, Krav tells me, and they glow in the dark.

I decide this is a good moment to try another question. "Can you tell me more about that estrus thing you mentioned?" They say forewarned is fore-armed.

"When an Alpha and an Omega are… well-suited, when their scents align, they can induce what we call rut and estrus in one another. They get aroused… desperately so… and are biologically ready to breed. The Omega produces slick…"

I bury my face in the moonflowers to hide the sudden rush of heat in my cheeks. I blush so dang easily.

"… and the Alpha forms a knot at the base of his cock."

"He doesn't usually have that?" I try to sound nonchalant, but my voice cracks. The sharp throb in my core doesn't help.

"No. Only with Omegas. It forms just before climax to bind them together, to make impregnation more likely." Krav sounds smug. "I'm sure you've felt mine."

"I wondered what it was," I say. "When you suddenly feel even… thicker." Embarrassed, I glare at him. "You can stop smirking now, please, and make me a mirror. One I can stand on this table."

"A mirror?"

"A glass to see yourself in." No wonder there isn't one anywhere to be found in this castle, if they don't exist here. Then I consider if that might not be a good thing. I haven't been able to keep up with my usual grooming routine out here, and for all I know, my skin is now paying the price.

"Why do you need that?" He sounds genuinely curious.

"For all kinds of reasons. To check I don't have spinach in my teeth. To do my hair. To put on makeup. I don't suppose you have any mascara, do you?" His mystified expression makes me giggle. "It's like a paste… to put on your eyelashes. To make them darker and, in my case, more visible." I feel naked without mascara. My lashes are long, but naturally strawberry blonde. When I'm not wearing makeup at all, I look like I don't have any.

Turning back to the flowers, I jump when he touches my shoulder. He can be insanely stealthy considering his size. "I can make your lashes darker, pet, but I don't know why you want me to. You're beautiful."

I slide my arms around his waist and look up at him. "Could you do that? Please?"

"Close your eyes," he says, and I obey, fighting back the usual rush of lust I get whenever he gives me an order.

There's a whisper, like a breeze, across my face, and something brushes my lashes as lightly as a butterfly wing.

"There," he says.

"I… I can't see myself." Duh. Should have thought of that. "Did you make—"

"Here." He hands me a mirror and I raise it tentatively to my face.

"Holy shit," I murmur. My lashes never looked so perfect before. Full, long, and a deep rich brown which enhances my eyes while still looking natural. "That's so, so incredible! And this mirror…" I turn it in my hand, examining it closely, "is exactly what I wanted. Thank you!" Instinctively, I go up on my tiptoes to kiss him.

Big mistake.

His hand curls in the hair at the base of my neck, gripping it, and his mouth comes down on mine with barely leashed ferocity. My knees turn to water and I almost drop the mirror.

For a few delicious seconds, I luxuriate in his kiss. It's dark and seductive, but I make myself pull back. "I want you too," I say gently, "but *please* can we finish this room first? We're almost done. And… maybe get something to eat?"

"You are denying me?" Krav is incredulous.

"No. I'm just asking if we can postpone." I get a sudden urge to lick his chest but force myself to resist. That would be giving mixed signals. "I know you use a little magic to *ease the path*, as it were, but I'm still made of flesh and blood. I'm human. I need a bit more recovery time." I raise an eyebrow. "Unless you can heal my pussy."

"Of course," he says, and reaches down.

I skip out of the way. "Let's do that—and each other— after I've put the curtains up and we've had a bite to eat."

His answering grin is predatory. "Do not presume to make demands of me, pet," he says slowly, folding his arms across his imposing chest. "While I enjoy indulging you, giving you things you want, never forget who I am: your Master. So I will offer you a choice. Either I rut you now, right here—and it can be quick, if you prefer—or we will wait until later, as you requested. But I warn you… if you choose to make me wait, there will be consequences. A forfeit. A price to be paid."

I lift my chin, determined not to show how hopelessly turned on I am by his threat. His nostrils flare, detecting my arousal, and I clench my thighs around my aching clit. "What kind of price?"

His glittering eyes have me mesmerized. "You'd have to wait and see. I promise it would be one you could pay… though it might not be easy."

Truthfully, I'm ready to let him fuck me again right here and now, but my endless curiosity is piqued and they do say that the best things come to those who wait. "I'll take the forfeit… Master," I add, knowing that addressing him that way drives him wild.

"Very well. We'll finish your nest, have some food, and then…"

"And then?" I ask when he trails off.

"And then I will take you to bed and show you what happens to naughty little Omegas who presume to command me."

My clit gives a long, languorous thump at his threat but I act unfazed. "And you'll heal me first?"

"Of course. I don't like to break my toys." His wink is deviant. "Just bend them a little."

SIX

Krav

I WAIT until my pet has eaten her fill of her favorite delicacies, including *leeberry* tarts and *kiktu* fruit. When she's finished, she wipes her lips on a cloth. The *jynx* swirl around to whisk the dishes away, and she flinches, but thanks them softly.

"You do not have to thank them," I say.

"It doesn't hurt to be kind."

"Kindness is weakness—when you're king." I hear the echo of my father's teachings in my words. "It is the way my kind have always ruled."

"Well, unlike you, I was raised to be polite," she retorts.

"Feisty today, are we?" I stand and stretch to my full height, towering above her. I'm bare-chested in leather breeches, my wings tucked behind me so only my horns rise above my head. "Perhaps I've been too kind to you. Perhaps I should remind you of your place, my pet." Reaching out, I draw her to her feet and take her to her room.

A flick of my claws and her gown falls to the floor to reveal her naked, glorious body. She flinches, but doesn't stop staring into my eyes. Her gaze is wide with anticipation —and need.

I run the back of my talon down her full breast.

Her expression is already glazed, her breath coming faster. It takes so little to arouse my sweet Omega. Perhaps I've been too easy on her. It's time to present her with a challenge.

"Are you ready for your forfeit, sweet one?"

She nods, biting her lip.

I step back until I'm across the room from her. The more the distance grows between us, the more nervous she looks. Once I've reached the wall, I beckon with a talon. "Crawl."

Red flags unfurl in her cheeks and she inhales sharply, but doesn't protest. She drops to her hands and knees and obeys. Her body undulates as she crawls towards me, her head tipped up, her back arched, and her ass waving in the air. Her breasts sway with the gentle movement. I would not allow her to do this on a stone floor and risk scraping her beautiful skin. The rug was a genius touch. Bless Omega nesting tendencies.

"I should carpet every room with furs. Make you crawl everywhere."

She's halfway across when I see the downside to my command. Her sensuous movements make my arousal build like lava at the base of my spine. She's crawling, but I'm the one in thrall.

"Stop," I order when she's a few feet away. "Turn around. Chest to the floor, present your cunt to me." How I love using crude language. How she loves to hear it. I'm ready to instruct her further, to ensure she stays on her hands and knees, but she executes the position perfectly. She presses her upper body to the rug, pushing her ass up further. I cannot see her expression but the tips of her ears are pink, clashing with her hair. This position makes her feel like the pet she is.

"Good girl," I praise her. "Keep your delectable ass in the air but spread your knees and arch your back so I can see every inch of you."

She does as I command, tilting her hips and presenting herself so I can see the slick glistening between her soft folds.

"Yes, that's it."

Her soft, coppery curls glint in the low light. I enjoy the fire-stone color of her hair, but it would be fun to shave that pussy bare.

"Reach between your legs." I order. "Touch yourself. No," I correct her when she tips her ass down. "Arch your back. Show me everything. This is for me, pet, not for you."

She obeys me, spreading her slick over her folds.

I crouch down, learning how she touches herself. She slides one slender finger into the groove between her inner and outer lips, and rubs her swelling clit. The slightest movement of her fingertip makes her twitch and shiver and sigh. I shift closer, my tail lashing the rug behind me, and she tenses, her ass clenching.

"Keep going."

She does, quivering under my perusal. Her fingertip slides higher, toward her entrance.

"No more, pet," I command. When she ignores me, I slap her buttock hard enough to make her gasp. "Hands down by your head."

Going to one knee behind her, I drag the tip of my throbbing cock up and down her folds. Her cunt is dripping slick and my cock is leaking as well. The musk of our arousal rises, blending together, making my head spin.

I breach her with the tip of my dick, the head stretching her tight, wet hole. When I pull out, she whimpers. If I were a kind Master, I'd give her what she's craving and fuck her into the floor, making her come over and over again. But as I told her, this is for me. "This is where I need you to be brave, sweetheart," I tell her. "Remember what I said—the forfeit might be difficult to bear but I know you can handle it. Do you trust me?"

She's panting, though I can't tell whether it's from fear or arousal. Maybe both. "Yes, Master."

"Good girl." I lean over her and slide my cock between her ass-cheeks. A few taps on her rear hole is enough to slicken it with my precum. I find the tiny target and press in gradually.

"Master," she cries, her fingers digging into the rug.

"Hush, you can take it," I croon, using magic to ease my path. Her ass is so incredibly tight. I can barely fit the head of my cock in and it's lava hot, like she's boiling inside.

I reach around her middle and graze her clit with a fingertip, gratified when she clenches around me.

"Shall I make you come like this? With the tip of my cock penetrating your ass?"

She moans and buries her face in the fur.

"I would use my magic." I'd have to. "I'd make it feel good. You're my little pet. You will give yourself to me in every way."

I rock my hips experimentally, and she tenses, but doesn't try to get away. *Good pet.* Slowly, I withdraw from her impossibly tight, tempting hole. "One day, you will yield your ass to me and take all of me here… but not yet."

I hold up my hand and call my magic. A bulb-shaped object appears in my palm. It's smooth and made of metal in the rose gold Renee loves so much, with a fire-stone jewel on the base.

"First, I want you to get used to wearing this for me." I hold the plug out to show her, my other hand caressing her hip. "Consider it training, of sorts. Of course, no amount of training would allow you to take all of me—only magic can do that. But the thought of you wearing this constant reminder of my ownership pleases me. Do you wish to please me?"

"Yes, Master," Renee whispers.

"That's my good girl." I slide the tapered bulb between her pussy folds, coating it with her slick. I use the tip to tickle her clit before positioning it at her asshole. She tenses. "Breathe," I remind her, and swivel the plug in.

A shuddering groan escapes her, and her head drops to the floor. But she opens for me, and soon the plug is seated between her plump ass-cheeks, the multi-faceted fire-stone winking enticingly.

"You'll keep this in all day, as a reminder of me, your Master. Remember this," I tap the jewel and she sucks in a breath, "when you would sass me."

I spank her ass lightly, over the plug, and delight in her startled cries. She sounds tormented, but when I go to check, her cunt soaks my hand.

"You love this, don't you? You love being my plugged and punished little pet."

Her hummed moan sounds like a denial, so I deliver several hard spanks to her right buttock.

"Admit it. Say, *Yes, Master. I love being your plugged pet.*"

Her reply is muffled by the rug.

I tug her up by her hair. "What was that?"

"Yes, Master," she repeats the phrase breathlessly. "I love being your plugged pet."

"Excellent. You look so beautiful like that, with one tight hole a glittering jewel, and the other dripping with need. Let's see if we can make it drip some more."

Getting up, I tug her forward, using her hair as a leash. She crawls behind me on her hands and knees until I make her rise and drape her front over the bed.

"That's better," I say. "Now I can spank you properly."

"Why?" she whispers.

"Because I want to. But if you really need a reason, we could call it a preemptive punishment." I set about slapping her ass, watching the skin turn deeper and deeper shades of pink. Renee's moans are muffled by the blankets but she's undulating her hips in the most delicious way. At length, I slide my hand between her spread thighs. Her pussy is gushing, soaking my palm.

"You're enjoying this. You should thank me for punishing you."

"Thank… you… Master."

"You can do better than that, sweet thing. Make me believe it. Or I won't give you a reward." My fingertip finds her clit, stroking it, and she lets out a groan.

"Thank you, Master. Your pet is so grateful for your punishment. Please, please, please… fuck me."

"You beg so beautifully." I stroke her hot pink flesh, gripping her ass and turning it this way and that so the jewel in her bottom flashes. Wanting to make her feel more helpless, I conjure a tether that secures her arms to the opposite side to the bed, and another that ties her legs together. "You want me to fuck you?"

"Please…"

Her round thighs make a lovely valley for me to fuck, especially with her slick soaking them. I guide my rigid, straining cock in there, my jaw clenched. I'm so close already.

"Please, Master. Please fuck my pussy," she sobs.

"Maybe I won't. Maybe I'll just fuck you like this, and leave your poor, needy cunt dripping for me. How does that sound?"

Her wails are music to me.

I fuck the crease between her legs until her inner thighs are pink and soaked with her slick. My tail snakes up to tap on the plug and she shudders as it pushes deeper into her delightful rear. My knot is forming. No longer able to hold off, I stand back and stroke myself in time to her pleas. The sight of her tied, spanked, and plugged is too much.

My wings unfurl with a snap and I roar as I paint her

back with my cum. As the pulsing waves of pleasure finally abate, I pause to admire the view, wishing I could preserve this moment in a painting. My naked pet, covered in my marks and seed. Her hair hides her face, sticking to skin made wet by her tears.

"Don't forget to thank me," I command.

She sniffles but says, "Thank you, Master, for your cum."

I caress her ass lightly with the tips of my talons. "You're welcome, my sweet Omega." She's still tied and so pretty, I can't keep my hands off her. "Such a good girl." My fingertip finds her rigid clit, and she gasps. The scent of her slick drives me mad.

I can't untie and leave her like this, sore and needy. She did all I asked of her and she did it well.

"You deserve a reward." I draw the plug out and push it back in. "This is how you'll climax." She lets out a long, moaning hum. Reaching between her legs, I finger her, fucking her with the plug all the while. Crouching down to better see what I'm doing, I whisper, "I'm going to train you to come whenever I fill your ass. Be it the plug or my cock, you'll learn to embrace the darkest pleasure. Pleasure only I can give..." She tenses at my words, and her breath comes in little pants. She's close. I use magic to elevate her body so I can taste her. She's dripping slick and I want to drink it all.

Starting at her clit, I sweep my tongue up, probing her pussy, then licking higher and higher. I draw the plug out with a pop and replace it with my tongue.

She screams and tenses. "Master, please may I?"

My fingertip finds her swollen clit as I growl to give her permission, my tongue still deep inside her tight ass. Her climax comes in a rush. I sink my thumb into her cunt to feel it clench in time with her back hole milking my tongue. I prolong the intimate kiss until her trembling subsides. Only when she's limp and drained do I replace the plug.

I swirl my tongue over her flesh, kissing the shiny pink

skin and the tiny bruises I put on her before removing the magic bonds and pulling her close on the bed.

Renee curls into a ball and I wrap myself around her, unfurling my right wing and spreading it over her.

Holding her like this feels right. I've never done this with anyone before—but then none of my previous bed-partners were Omegas. That must be why it feels different with Renee.

"Thank you, Master," she murmurs, half asleep.

"You're welcome, my pet." I'm answered by a tiny snore. A deep sense of relaxation rolls over me, but I fight it and extricate myself carefully.

There's a twinge, deep in my chest. I rub my breastbone until it's gone.

After rearranging my clothes, I head for the door, then pause again. Somewhere in the castle, someone is weeping. I hesitate, a summons to my servants on the tip of my tongue before I realize I'm hearing a memory. It's not real.

The only thing real here is Renee—as fantastical as her presence might seem.

Although I long to stay, it wouldn't do to make a habit of sleeping with my pet. Even though she is my Omega, she must remember her place.

And I must remember mine.

SEVEN

Krav

MY LITTLE PET IS RESTLESS. Maybe it's the plug in her ass—a new one, with a bigger fire-stone jewel. I bend her over at times, ostensibly to check if it's still there. She fusses but cannot deny the slick that leaks from her when I use it to fuck her forbidden hole.

Right now, she's pacing up and down my great hall, pestering me with questions. Ulf knows, the Hoo-man always has so many questions.

"Do you know why those people in the village tied me to a tree for you? Why they felt the need to appease you?" she asks, gesturing to one of the enormous windows.

I shrug. "No."

"They said something about you stealing women and girls from the kingdom. They're afraid of you."

"As they should be." I admire the way her curves are visible beneath the gossamer gown I designed and created especially for her luscious body. The fabric is so sheer, it hides nothing, yet wearing it gives her the sense of being covered. While I'm no longer actively in rut, my lust for her is still profound.

"So you did? Take the women? And… girls?"

Her horrified tone makes me stop comparing her nipples to *leeberries* and glance up at her face. "Of course not. I'm not a thief. Nor am I unnecessarily cruel. Whenever I required… female company—" her eyes narrow and I hasten to add, "—*before* you arrived, my pet—I made sure to find a *willing* participant."

The Omega is jealous. How adorable. Tossing her hair over her shoulder, she turns her back on me and pretends to be interested in the lake.

I continue, "I am glad that is no longer necessary. Now, I have you."

There's a long pause. I consider telling her that every other female I had before her pales by comparison. Not because they were bad but because she is spectacular. A genuine Omega. The first to send me into rut. The first I have knotted. The first I wish to keep.

"Are you pouting, my pet?"

She ignores my question. "If you didn't take them… who did?"

"In all likelihood, it was the Stone King. He was obsessed with the idea of finding a mate. A queen. An Omega. We Alphas do love our Omegas."

She mutters something I don't catch.

"What was that?"

"Nothing." She sounds petulant. My palm itches to spank her, but I do enjoy her little flashes of defiance. Always a good excuse to punish her later. "If you knew it was the Stone King, did you do anything to stop him?"

I examine my claws. "The Stone King's power was based on rot and decay. Pyreda has natural defenses to such magic. He only would have been able to successfully lure females to him via some form of deception. In other words, they would have made a deliberate choice to leave."

Moving away from the window, she comes over to face me, her arms crossed over her chest. "That's a fancy way of saying you didn't do anything."

"In all honesty, I did not know he was luring females away." I might have, if I had heeded the missives from my subjects, but Renee doesn't need to know that. "He was obsessed with the thought of finding a mate. A queen. An Omega. As long as I've been alive, there have been rumors of hidden Omegas—Ulfarri Omegas—who went underground to avoid being taken by Alphas against their will. He would have been targeting them."

"And you let him."

Getting out of my chair, I rise to my full height, towering over the tiny Hoo-man. The shadow my wings cast swallows her whole body. "Pyreda is unconquerable. Only a demon can rule this land of smoke and fire. My power is absolute." Ulf, I sound like my father.

Renee scoffs, unfazed. "It's obviously not, if you let women get deceived by some shitty king."

Bristling, I glare down at her. "The Stone King is dead, and his search for Omegas died with him. Not to mention, it would be impossible to control all my subjects' actions."

"But you could do your job as ruler. I can't say I've seen you do any form of governing while I've been here. Nor do I see any councilors or other staff doing it for you. Why be king if you're not gonna rule?"

I sink back into my chair to disguise my rising temper. "The world is harsh. Cruel. Unforgiving. Only strength will save you. My father taught me that coddling and indulging your subjects leads to ruin. They grow weak, incapable of fending for themselves. Worse, they get demanding, greedy… I won't have Pyreda filled with petulant children."

"They didn't seem like petulant children to me." Renee

wrinkles her speckled nose. She refers to her markings as *freckles*. "Just scared. Scared of the threats you won't protect them from, and scared of you."

"As they should be." I dig my claws into the ancient carved armrests, fighting to keep my voice level.

The Omega's eyes are curious, unafraid. Who does she think she is, to make such accusations? Does she have no idea how close I am to pouncing on her? "Do you at least keep an eye on *your* subjects?" she asks. "Make sure they have enough food? Keep them safe from that volcano?" She gestures to the window that frames Mount Vracor. It hasn't smoked or rumbled since I accepted her as my gift. But it's far from dormant. Even now, I feel the fire in its belly, churning like my own emotions.

My father would never have tolerated this sort of interrogation from anyone, not even his mate. He would have had Renee sobbing and begging by now.

Why haven't I done the same?

In a faraway corner of my mind, I hear a melancholy twang. It sounds like someone weeping. My gut lurches. A premonition of my pet's face, twisted and soaked with tears, makes me want to claw at my chest.

Gritting my teeth, I shove the mental image aside. I am king. I will not be interrogated.

"Why do your questions always lead to more questions?" I counter. "And you wonder why I'm loath to answer any of them. This is why!"

She lifts her chin in a gesture of defiance, exposing her throat. There's a sharp ache in my canines and I lick them to soothe it.

"I'm warning you, pet," I tell her. "So far, you've enjoyed all the ways in which I've punished you, but none were real *punishments*. Yet."

She takes a tiny step back, unaware of the way that always triggers my hunting instinct.

I'm quivering with outrage. Tension. Lust. "And let's not forget you're no longer in estrus. I've refrained from fucking you since your heat ended because I'm not sure you'll be able to handle it if you're not making as much slick. Maybe I've just been too courteous. Too indulgent with you. Perhaps I should just throw you to the ground and shove my big, hard cock inside you, regardless of whether or not you enjoy it."

Her eyes are huge now, her little fists clenching and unclenching at her sides. But I've seen that expression before. As always, my threats are arousing her even if she fights against her body's reaction to my dominance. "You can't bully me," she declares at length. "And I don't know what you're getting so mad about. I was just asking questions."

"That's what I'm—" I close my eyes and take a deep breath, wrestling my ire back under control. When I next speak, my voice is calmer even though I don't feel it. Time to regain the upper hand by using her own tactics against her. "Are you not happy here?"

"I..." She pauses and bites her lip. "Is that a serious question?"

"Of course."

"What do *you* think? How would *you* feel if you were in my situation? You just woke up one day on a different freaking planet, and a bunch of weird strangers decided to give you to their queen—who took one look at you, and made you her sex slave?"

I scoff. "I would never allow it."

She cocks her head, studying me. "Not even if she was much bigger? More powerful? A sorceress, perhaps?"

"The mere notion is ridiculous."

"Jesus!" Renee throws up her arms. "It's a hypothetical situation. You know? Where you put yourself in someone else's place? Ever heard of empathy?"

"Why would I put myself in someone else's place?" I'm genuinely baffled by the notion. "Is this something you do?"

"I would go so far as to say most people—humans, at any rate—have at least a degree of empathy, yes. Some more than others. But unless they're sociopaths, everyone has the capacity to appreciate how they might feel if they were in someone else's situation. I don't need to see my own house burn down to understand how fucking awful it would be to lose everything. To comprehend the fear, loss, devastation I would feel if it happened to me."

I let her words sink in, turning the statement over in my mind.

"You've never thought about it, have you?" Her tone is no longer accusatory. If anything, she sounds astonished. "It's an entirely foreign concept to you."

"I'm a demon. We don't spend much time considering *feelings*." I rub at my chest. The ache under my breastbone has returned.

My beautiful Omega sinks to the floor in a single graceful movement. Now she's sitting just beyond my clawed feet, her legs crossed at the ankles, her expression one of endless curiosity. I tense, anticipating yet another question. Instead, she says, "That's a shame. And it explains a lot."

"What do you mean?" Her accusatory tone makes me bristle.

"Your wall. Ever since I arrived, you've had this wall up." She gestures at my chest. "There's this... invisible barrier, making it impossible to get close to you."

This time, I can't hold back my snort of disbelief. "You've been closer to me than anyone else ever has. I've been inside you countless times—"

"I don't mean the sex... or physical proximity. I mean... ugh, how do you explain emotional vulnerability to a freaking *demon*?" Exasperated, she shoves her hair over her shoulder. "What about love?"

"Love," I echo.

"Yes! Please tell me at least that's a thing here."

I shrug. "I have no need of it."

"Of course you do. Everybody does."

I shift in my chair, trying to get comfortable. There's a rush of air and a *jynx* unfurls beside me, like a plume of harnessed smoke. Renee scoots back, always wary of my shadow servants. For once, I'm grateful for the interruption.

"What does it want?" she asks as I'm listening to the message.

Getting to my feet, I pause, wondering whether to include her. "My pet—Plutus—has returned," I admit. "Would you like to meet him?"

She chews her lip, then holds out her hand for me to help her up off the floor. Her fingers are cold to the touch and I grip them tight. "Ouch," she mutters. "A little more awareness of your own strength would be appreciated." I glare at her and she hastens to add, "And yes please, I'd love to meet Plutus."

At least my little Omega has the good sense to know when a conversation has run its natural course. Sometimes. "Then let's go."

Renee

If that wasn't the most infuriating dang conversation anybody ever had... and then we got interrupted right when it was getting interesting. I'm so distracted, and not just by the plug in my ass—unsettling though it may be. There's a restlessness in me, a deep need to find out about every aspect of Krav's life. To learn everything about him. But for now, I'll settle for getting to see his mysterious pet.

Trudging along the hallways behind him, I keep stealing glimpses at Krav's broad back. His gleaming wings are magnificent even when they're tucked away, like now.

So demons *don't do* love, huh? I've heard some paltry excuses from commitment-phobes before but this is a new one. Still, it would explain a lot. Like the fact that he just won't be affectionate with me. He never cuddles me for long, not even after sex. If I'm cold, he'll haul me up against him until I stop shivering, then he's quick to move away.

Nor did I understand the whole separate bedroom arrangement until now. The first time I fell asleep beside him after sex, I woke up in a different bed. Alone. In what is now my room.

Sometimes, I wake up and sense him pacing around my bed. But he never climbs in, and I always fall back asleep.

It would be nice to be held while I sleep, but on the other hand, I'm grateful for the reprieve—it's a relief to get the occasional break from being horny, and I'm always horny around him. Also, having lived alone for several years now, I don't think I would deal real well with being around someone else 24/7. Especially a stranger. An *alien* stranger. Who, as it turns out, has the emotional intelligence of a twenty-something fuckboi.

We reach a huge, heavy door, which opens as if by magic. Maybe it is. "I don't see a handle," I say, hoping Krav will tell me how it works. I get anxious in places I can't exit easily.

"There's a tile," he says, indicating it with his foot. "Just step on the tile and the door opens. There's one on the other side too, of course."

"Ah. Thank you." The door doesn't need to be held but Krav gallantly waits until I've gone through it before following me out.

I once had a job where my slightly older, male supervisor held a door for me, then informed me that guys only do that so they can check out your ass as you pass by them. Weird how little memories like that resurface occasionally. Especially now, when I can't even remember the name of my street back home.

A cold breeze nips my face as soon as I'm outside, and I shiver in the ridiculous cobweb Krav calls a dress. The newly discovered submissive part of me doesn't mind wearing what he wants—I'd go so far as to admit I enjoy it—but now we're outside, I'm rapidly changing my stance.

I inch closer to Krav. His skin burns hotter than a human's. He may not be a huge fan of cuddling or intimacy, but too bad. I need him to be my seven-foot-tall heater.

"You're cold," he says. "Wait." He does that blurry thing with his hands, making it rain silver sparks, then gives me a fur-lined cloak which I tug gratefully around my shoulders.

"Thanks," I tell him. At least I don't have to worry about animal cruelty, what with it being man-made. Well. Demon-made. I suppress a grin at my own silly joke.

The air carries a hint of frost, completely at odds with the expanse of boiling, bubbling lava which surrounds the castle. The volcano looks dormant, and the three suns are low in the sky. If they're giving off any warmth at all, I can't feel it. What are the seasons like here? Not that long ago, I was tied to a tree and freaking out about getting sunburn. Now it smells like winter.

"Does it snow here?" I ask Krav, who's peering across the lake like he's searching for something.

"Snow?"

"Cold, white stuff falling from the sky. Big feature of Christmas cards, and the Winter Olympics." Of course, he wouldn't know what Christmas is. I should tell him sometime.

"We—" His voice is drowned out by an eldritch shriek which raises every last tiny hair on my body. I instinctively press myself up against Krav who, after a second, puts his arm around me. His scent is like hot cocoa by a bonfire on a cold evening. With marshmallows. And whisky.

Together, we watch the sky.

"Don't make eye contact with him until I tell you to," Krav murmurs. "Otherwise he'll take it as a sign of aggression."

"And then what would happen?" I squeak. It didn't occur to me to be afraid of Plutus… until now.

"Then he'd—here, Plutus, come to me!" There's another ear-splitting screech, like from a barn owl the size of a T-rex, and I'm so anxious about accidentally making eye-contact that I bury my face in Krav's chest as Plutus approaches.

A great gust of wind and a frantic rustling of wings later, Krav turns around, moving me with him. "I'm just shutting him in," he tells me. "You can open your eyes but don't look directly at Plutus's face until I say."

I keep my gaze trained firmly on the ground as we approach. The obsidian rock beneath our feet is soon interrupted by an industrial metal frame—the door to the cage.

"Stop here," Krav orders. His arm slides off my shoulders, the weight lifting, leaving me oddly bereft—and colder. There are grating noises, like bolts being driven home, then he tugs me back against him. Weird how his arm around me feels so right. "Plutus, meet Renee," Krav announces. "My *other* pet." I roll my eyes. "Sweetheart, now you can look all you like."

"Holy shit," I breathe. Plutus is magnificent. Around ten feet tall, he stands on huge green talons tipped with razor-sharp claws. He has the feet, head and wings of a predatory bird, and the body and tail of a great cat. "A real, live griffin!"

"Griffin?"

"A mythical creature back home." Plutus tosses his head and prances back and forth as I admire his striking turquoise and gold plumage.

"Mythical?"

"Yeah. One that doesn't exist. Like unicorns, dragons…" *Men who keep their vows.*

"They don't exist… and yet they have names, and you know what they look like?"

Now that I think about it, I can see how that statement would baffle Krav. "Doesn't matter," I say. "I can always explain it later." Right now I'm too busy gawking at the animal in front of me with a mixture of awe and intimidation. I don't know what I expected when Krav first mentioned Plutus to me, but it certainly wasn't this. "What did you say he is?"

"A *styxian*," Krav says, a note of pride in his voice. "Very rare."

As if to prove that point, Plutus rears up and snorts, twin lilac flames spiraling out of the holes in his beak. "Jesus!" Even though there's a barrier between us, I take a step back. Krav's arm tightens around me. "He spits fire?"

"He's posturing. Those little flames are as much as he can do. More a threatening gesture than an attack mechanism."

Plutus cocks his head. His piercing honey stare is intense. Unblinking as a snake's. "Wow." Not sure I want to know the answer, I ask anyway. "How does he attack then, if not with fire?"

"His talons." Krav indicates the creature's huge feet. "They can disembowel a fully grown Ulfarri Alpha before he can blink. *Styxian* have lightning-quick reflexes."

I'm reminded of the velociraptor claw scene from Jurassic Park, where the little boy makes the mistake of telling Dr. Grant the dinosaur skeleton looks like an overgrown turkey. Only this isn't a movie.

"Want to feed him?" Krav asks.

"Depends… what with?"

Krav lets go of me and makes for a chest I didn't notice before. Tugging open the lid, he removes a dark blue, scaly thing about the size of a mouse.

Plutus snorts again and rustles his wings.

"*Crius*," Krav says, holding it out. I approach cautiously.

"Ew! It's a critter!"

Krav chuckles as I recoil. "Ulf only knows why Plutus likes them so much, but he's crazy for them," he says, tossing the dead thing through the bars.

Plutus snatches it out of the air and swallows it whole, chittering with excitement.

"That's all he eats?" I raise an eyebrow. "When he's that big?"

"Oh no. He hunts and feeds himself whenever he goes out. Don't you?" Krav tosses several more blue critter-corpses into the cage before closing and locking the chest.

"What does he hunt?" Do I want to know? What if this animal was responsible for some of the kids going missing?

Krav shrugs. "Whatever he can find."

"Does that include people? Ulfarri?" It's still so surreal that people are called that here.

"If he feels threatened. He doesn't eat them."

"That's good." I glance sideways at Krav. My demon lover. The previous tension between us has faded, leaving only a comfortable warmth. He's not even cranky about my questions—although that's probably because none of his answers about Plutus require any kind of internal reflection. "How did you get him?"

"He appeared right here one day, as a youngling," Krav says. "He was screeching so loudly, I could hear him from my room. His wing was injured. I healed him."

"With magic?"

He nods. "After making sure he could fly again, I let him go... but he kept coming back. Eventually, it was clear he had decided he lives here now, so I made him this cage. It's more to give him shelter than to keep him locked up. As a child, I always wanted a pet."

"Your parents didn't allow you one?"

"Oh no. If my sire had been alive, he would have killed Plutus on sight. Or had the *jynx* do it."

I shiver. The little hints Krav drops about his father make me think he wasn't a nice guy. Cold. Selfish. An all-round terrible dad… and king.

Krav seems to think he should follow in his father's footsteps, and he does… but occasionally I get glimpses of how kind and gentle he can be. Like now.

Reaching between the bars, Krav scratches the top of Plutus's head, ruffling the short, spiky feathers, and in that instant, it hits me.

I'm falling for the demon.

Goddamnit.

EIGHT

ON OUR WAY back inside the castle, Renee fills the silence with chatter.

"Females should be seen and not heard," my father once told me. He believed the same of his progeny, only summoning me when he felt the need to pass on a bit of paternal wisdom.

Did my mother try to fill the silence between us, as Renee does now? My memories of her are vague, faded over time, but I do recall the grace with which she moved, and the elegance with which she carried herself, whether taking a stroll, or playing haunting melodies on the *hriox*, her preferred instrument. She was tall for an Omega, and impossibly slender. My father was gigantic by comparison. Another reason to wonder how they made me.

Renee's ass sways as she walks ahead of me. It's so plump, so enticing, even when I'm not in rut. I'm glad I made her remove the cloak the moment we got back inside. The firestone jewel between her cheeks winks at me through her gauzy gown.

Striding down the corridors, heading for the main hall, she's babbling about *myths* and *unicorns* and something called a *onesie*. I could command her to be silent, but her one-sided conversation is endearing.

Is this constant need to talk and ask questions a Hoo-man thing? Do Ulfarri females behave this way? For the first time, it occurs to me that there are other kings I could ask about these things. Khan, Aurus, the Hunter King—even that disfigured Bestian—have all claimed Hoo-man Omegas. Did they ever compare research? Turn to one another for advice?

Suppressing a sigh, I dismiss the idea. I have no need of guidance. Renee is my pet, not my queen. She does as I command, either of her own volition, or when I make her. And thankfully her instinctive reaction to any display of dominance from me, her Master, is to stay her tongue.

A surge of heat rushes through my groin when I recall her response to my threat to take her even though she's not in estrus. The look in her eyes was exquisite. While it's true she will likely not produce as much slick as when she's in heat, the rest was said to intimidate her. I will always ensure she can handle me, even if she doesn't know I'm doing it.

We've reached the great hall and she turns to me. "I'm thirsty," she says.

"I expect you would be, my pet. Since we left Plutus, you've barely drawn a breath."

She wrinkles her nose. "I have to do something to distract myself from this plug."

I chuckle. "It's not the plug you wish to forget. It is your response to it."

Her face turns pink but she ignores what I said, proving my point. "Could we please have something to drink?"

"Of course. There's juice over there." I point to the jug on the table.

"Do you have any hot drinks here?" My confusion must be obvious because she adds, "You know, tea, coffee, cocoa?"

"Tea… like medicine?" I summon a *jynx*.

"No! Well, I mean, we do have herbal teas back home, but I meant more the other kind. Chai. English. Green."

Once again, I have no idea what she's babbling on about. But she is my pet and I wish to indulge her every whim, so I ask her to describe one of her favorite beverages to me. I cannot make it myself, since nothing created with magic should be swallowed, but perhaps the *jynx* can find something similar.

"Do y'all have chocolate over here?" she says at length. "It's made from the cocoa bean. Brown, sweet, creamy. Delicious. We like to drink it in hot liquid form, topped with whipped cream and marshmallows. I… no, I can't describe those. Squishy. Sweet. Fluffy."

"Whipped cream?"

"Oh god. It's… semi-solid whipped milk. Maybe this is a mistake. I don't want you to bring me butter! Way too much room for interpretation—and error."

The *jynx* was listening intently, and I tell it to see what it can find. "And bring some *kasewl* with it, just in case," I add as the servant whooshes off. "In the meantime, you should have some juice," I tell Renee. "To slake your thirst."

"Thanks." She takes the jug and pours some into a cup, drinking greedily. It reminds me of the first day I brought her back here. It was such a short while ago, yet in some ways, it feels like a lifetime.

"Is there anything else you need, sweet one?" I ask as Renee sets the empty cup down and wipes her mouth with the back of her hand.

"Actually, yes. I've been thinking." She pauses, watching me intently.

"I'm listening."

"Well. You know you mentioned there were other humans here? Who were turned into Omegas?"

"Did I?"

"Nice try. You know you did. I was wondering if there was a way to contact them."

"Why?"

"So I could talk to them. I have so many questions, and it would be good to talk to someone who understands."

I rub my chest. "You think I do not understand?"

"I know you don't. You admitted you don't have empathy, remember?" Her smile is rueful.

Oh, for the love of Ulf. Not this again. "You do not need to talk to the other Omegas," I tell her. "Besides, I wouldn't know how to arrange it."

She cocks her head. "You're lying."

"What makes you think that?" While it's true, the accusation irks me.

"Your horns turn green," she says with an infectious giggle.

My lips curve up, my chest instantly lighter. "Now who's lying?" In three strides, I'm directly beside her. "You should remember that naughty little pets who lie get punished."

A pink stain creeps up her cheeks and her breathing quickens. "Don't. Not now."

"Don't what?" I reach out and slide a hand over the curve of her ass before tugging her up against me, pressing her belly against my thighs. She lets out a gratifying gasp.

"Turn me on. I'm trying to have a real conversation, and it's so hard to think straight when you…"

My other hand cups her breast, my thumb caressing her nipple through the sheer fabric of her gown. "When I…" I prompt.

"When you… do that stuff. Act all dominant. Remember we had that conversation about BDSM the other day?"

"Ah, yes. You told me that some Hoo-mans enjoy tying each other up and whipping each other so much that there are entire books written on the subject."

"Really? *That* was your main takeaway?"

I begin to rock against her, slowly, gently, letting her feel how hard I am. She gives the tiniest whimper. "I was intrigued by all of it. The symbolism—how a mere collar can be so significant. The way you said that not all Hoo-mans like it—and there are varying levels among those who do. And of course the fact that some females take the dominant role—which is just incomprehensible to me."

"It is? What's so surprising about that?"

I shrug. "All females should submit to their mates."

She tries to pull away but my hand on her butt keeps her pressed up against me. "That's ridiculous!" Her voice quivers.

"Ulfarri females are naturally submissive—at least sexually," I clarify. "And for good reason. Alphas are bigger and stronger in every possible way. And when the rut overcomes them, things can get a little violent… as you know." I pinch her nipple, and her gasp of pleasure is immediate. "This way, they can still enjoy it."

"The difference is consent," Renee says. "Having a choice."

"There's always a choice," I tell her. My hand leaves her buttock and creeps down, tapping the jewel of the plug gently through the gauzy fabric. "You can choose whether to obey or disobey. Whether to enjoy it… or not. Whether to come…" wedging my thigh against her crotch, I grind against her sex until she sucks in a breath and tenses up before taking a step back, "…or not."

Her hands tighten against my chest. "Goddamnit, that's so—"

"Ah," I interrupt, letting her go and turning to the *jynx* who just appeared behind us. "The drinks have arrived."

Renee looks warily at the cups on the table. Recognizing the *kasewl*, I pick up the other one and sniff it before passing it over.

"Well," my pet says, peering at it, "I guess my descriptions of cream and marshmallows were too much for the *jynx*. And it certainly doesn't smell like chocolate. Or coffee. Or anything else I've ever encountered, come to think of it."

My eye twitches. "Even so… are you going to try it?"

"Sure, why not? I've tried everything else you've given me so far." Her wink immediately soothes some of the irritation building in me. "I even liked most of it."

I watch her sip the hot liquid. Her beautiful face contorts for an instant before she graces me with the biggest false smile. "Well?" I ask.

"I've gotta say that's a *no* for the local cocoa. But I do appreciate the gesture. Honestly I do. What's that other one?" She sets down her cup and reaches for the *kasewl*.

"It's fermented, made from a sweet local root."

Peering into the cup, she raises an eyebrow. "Looks like pondwater. Hope it tastes better than it smells!" Then, after a taste, "Holy moly! It…" she smacks her lips, "it's kinda like *funnel cake*. How can that be?"

It's also a powerful aphrodisiac but I want to wait a while before informing her about that little tidbit. "Do you like it?"

"Hell yeah I do!" She swallows the rest, tipping her head back, and as I watch her throat work, an idea forms in my mind. Placing the cup back on the tray, she turns to face me and tilts her head to one side. Her gaze is serious. "I want to get back to what we were talking about before."

I raise an eyebrow.

"The other humans," she clarifies. "You keep saying you want to give me whatever I want. I know you mean jewels and clothes and—" she waves at the tray behind her, "—you try to give me things I miss from home. And I appreciate all that, I do. But what I'm craving is answers to my questions. I'd take a chance to chat with one of these girls over the best cocoa in the galaxy."

Her plea is sweet, sincere, but a stab of panic lances my chest nonetheless. Renee belongs to me. What if they turn her against me? Or put other silly notions in her head? My father never allowed my mother to mingle with other queens. An icy prickle of dread tingles along my spine. What if they've found a way to get her home? "No," I say firmly, crossing my arms.

Her eyes widen. "That's it? Just no?"

"Exactly. No."

A gamut of different expressions flicker across her face. She's casting about, working out how best to respond. "But… where's the harm?" Her lower lip pooches out. "I just want to talk to them. One of them? I'd be happy with one!"

Rapidly losing my patience, I resort to something that never fails: I let out a low growl.

Renee gasps and takes a step back. Her pulse is fluttering in her throat. "Goddamnit," she whispers. "I didn't think that would work when I'm not in estrus…"

I suppress a smirk. "Come to the bedroom with me." I extend a hand to her. "I have a surprise for you."

"I thought you said we couldn't… that it wouldn't fit if—"

"I will make it fit. Magic, remember?"

"Oh. Yeah." Still, she hesitates.

For some reason, it's important to me that she comes willingly, so as much as I want to pounce on her and carry her to my bed, I wait, my hand still extended in invitation. "I'm going to count to three. If you haven't taken my hand by then, I will leave you be," I tell her. "Your choice. One…"

She licks her lips. "You'll *leave me be?* What does that mean?"

"Let you have some time to yourself. I'll still be here in the castle. Two…"

Her eyes are wide with confusion but I can scent her arousal. It's much fainter than during estrus but it's there. It's been a while since she's had any form of release, and the aphrodisiac must be working by now. I take a breath to say *three*, and she places her palm in mine.

Hiding my relief, I draw her to me, my hands traveling

over her curves. My tail swishes around her waist to pull her closer. "That's my good pet. Let's adjourn to the bedroom so I can relieve this…" my fingertip slips between her thighs, drawing slow circles over the rigid bud of her clit, "ache."

Renee gasps and clutches me. "Yes please… Master."

As always, her use of that word floods my chest with warmth. "Good girl."

My good girl.

Mine.

Renee

I must be under some kind of spell. Until tonight, I had put my newly discovered pleasure in submission down to this Omega estrus thing.

But I'm not in estrus anymore, and yet when that demon growled, I almost came on the spot.

Then he confused me more by asking me to go to bed with him. Krav never asks. He orders. He takes. He commands. Is this new show of respect because of the recent conversation we had about consent? Or is it because he's no longer in rut?

While I'm desperate to continue making my case for meeting the other Earth women—or at least one of them—I'm old enough to know when to keep pushing a subject, and when to bide my time. In that regard, Krav is easy to read. So I'll drop the topic. For now.

Besides, it'll be way easier to have a conversation when my ass isn't filled with this plug.

Of course I was going to choose to satisfy my curiosity about this surprise he has in store for me. For a wicked demon, he's awfully generous. Will his surprise be sweet? Cruel? A delicious combination of both?

My temperature is rising to match his. I'm not in heat but I'm insanely hot for him again… still… whatever.

Once we're in my bedroom, he says "Strip," in a tone that turns my knees to water.

My dress slips easily over my head. Krav designed it that way.

His tail lashes the air behind him, but the rest of him remains still. Cold. Imperious. And damn if that doesn't turn me on. "Kneel down and close your eyes."

The floor is hard even through the rug. I shift from knee to knee, hoping it won't be long before we move to the soft mattress. The plug feels bigger in this position.

"Who owns you?" His words are accompanied by a growl which makes my entire pussy clench—just once, but violently.

"You do, Master."

"Which is why I want you to wear this. Open your eyes."

I blink, bringing the glittering object in his outstretched palm into focus. It's a collar. Fashioned in gleaming rose gold, it's made of three twirled cords, delicately interwoven. A tiny, flame-colored gemstone sparkles in the center. I swallow, my throat suddenly dry. "It's stunning," I croak.

"You like it?" The hope in his voice is endearing.

"I do. It's beautiful."

"And yet not as beautiful as you."

The warmth in his voice stirs my belly. When he talks like this, I melt into a puddle of goo.

"Lift your hair, pet."

I lower my head and gather the hair off the nape of my neck as he moves behind me. The metal is smooth and comforting against my skin. "Thank you," I whisper once he's fastened it into place.

"I want to give you all the pretty things," he murmurs, leaning down and helping me to my feet. His hand trails down over my belly, lower… lower… but just before he gets to my thrumming clit, he reaches to cup my cheek instead. "Now get on the bed. On your back."

I love it when he gives me direct orders. Of course, I also love it when he's too impatient and positions me himself. I do as he says, heat pulsing through my core. In my aroused state, even the plug in my ass feels good. Seems I'm discovering an anal kink as well as a submissive side.

"Spread your legs wide, and close your eyes. Arms above your head."

Within moments, he's tied me down, my wrists and ankles secured to the four posts. My heart is racing with anticipation, and that familiar prickle of fear I always get when Krav seduces me.

My clit feels huge, throbbing painfully.

Krav joins me on the bed, the mattress dipping beneath his weight. I hold my breath.

"Look at you, stretched out and naked, tied down and helpless," he murmurs. His fingertip trails up my leg and I shiver. "My beautiful pet. I can do anything I like to you, isn't that right?"

His caress whispers over my belly and up toward my breast. "Yes," I breathe.

There's a savage pain in my nipple. He's twisting it. "Yes what?"

"Yes, Master."

Immediately, the ache fades as he lets go. "Good girl." He lets his huge hands wander, skating over every inch of my skin, touching me everywhere except where I want it the most. Something prods the plug in my ass—the tip of his tail. Each tap makes my pussy gush as if there's a direct line from my stretched back-hole to my pleasure centers. I grit my teeth to fight my growing arousal.

"You're trembling," he says, "are you cold?"

"No," I huff. "You know that's not why I'm shaking."

His dark chuckle rumbles through me. "Do you think

now is a good time to sass me, pet? When you're so completely at my mercy, unable to defend yourself?"

Goddamnit, why do his threats always have this effect on me? "You're so much bigger than I am, I don't think I could defend myself against you anyhow," I retort. "Besides, I can't help being sassy. Especially when you tease me like this."

"You think this is teasing?" Another dark chuckle. "Oh, sweet thing, this is nothing."

I'm trying to find a snarky reply when his tongue finds my clit, and I arch my hips at the sudden jolt of pleasure. "Oh!"

I'm so, so close but instead of letting me come, he licks every square inch of available flesh between my legs until I'm dripping wet, and begging.

"Please, Master, please, please..."

"Not yet. Not for a long time yet. After all, you're not in estrus. I need to make sure you're completely ready before I rut you."

"I *am* ready! I swear!" We both know he can use his magic to ease his path if necessary. He's just making excuses to drive me out of my mind. And I hate and adore it in equal measure.

His tongue delves under the hood of my clit for an excruciatingly brief, delicious second, then vanishes.

"Fuck!" I howl. A sharp slap to my thigh is his response. As it always does, the sting magnifies the pleasure when he twirls the entrance to my pussy with a single fingertip.

"Not nearly wet enough," he says, "but luckily, I have just the thing. Keep your eyes closed, pet, or I'll make you wish you had. I could just leave you tied up here like this all night."

"You wouldn't dare!" I say with a little more conviction than I feel. I freaking hope he wouldn't do that. I don't think I'd survive it. I squeeze my eyes more tightly shut.

"Have you ever known me not to follow through on a threat?"

"Not yet," I concede. Then again, I haven't known him that long.

"Then I would suggest you don't test me." There's a pause before something hard and smooth presses against my straining clit. "There," he says, as if talking to himself, "that should be the right place. Now to make sure it stays on." The pressure increases, followed by firm strokes along the insides of my thighs and up over my mons.

"Master, what are you—"

"Hush, sweetheart. This is an old trick used by kings of days gone by to help keep their courtesans... interested in their advances."

"I'm not a courtesan! And I *am* interested in your advances. I don't need any—"

The sudden vibrations against my entire pussy cut off my ability to speak. To think. To breathe. I go rigid as the buzzing gets stronger... stronger... then it stops. I open my mouth to howl with frustration—and it starts again. Gentle... more... more... again, it cuts off just as I'm about to go over the edge.

"Jesus, fuck, please!" I whimper, twisting my hips in a futile attempt to change the setting, make the thing fall off me, anything to stop the torment.

Krav's finger once again finds my entrance, sliding in just the tiniest bit. My pussy walls flutter with unfulfilled longing. "Hm," he says in the most infuriatingly casual tone, "it seems to be working. I think a little more time with this will get you wet enough for me."

"I *am* wet enough!" I manage when the vibrator cuts out for what feels like the millionth time already. It starts again and I bite my lip. "Please. I can't take any more of this. I need to—"

"You need to do nothing but lie here and take it," he growls, his voice suddenly directly in my ear. His tail brushes my leg and goosebumps shiver across my skin. "Lie here like a good little pet, like *my* good little pet, and let the pleasure wash over you, building and building… until I come back to relieve it. I own you. I own your pleasure. And I own your release."

"But Master—"

"One more word of complaint, and I will make good on my threat to leave you here like this all night. Is that what you want?"

I shake my head.

"Open your eyes."

I blink to see his dark, hungry gaze just inches away.

"You can take this for me, sweetheart. And you will. It won't be for long—although it might feel like it. And when I return, I will make you come so hard, you'll pass out."

My lower belly clenches. My butt squeezes around the rigid plug, sending sensation pulsing through me, adding a darker layer to my arousal.

"Besides," his lips curve into a predatory smile, "it's not like you aren't enjoying it, even if you won't admit it. I know your every expression. And while your mouth likes to protest, your eyes tell the truth. A deep, hungry part of you is loving every moment of this delicious torture. Isn't that right?"

The vibrations crescendo, halt, and resume building once again before I'm able to speak. "Yes, Master." It's annoying how he's always right about this. That he knows me better sexually than I know myself.

Annoying—and so, so good.

"Good girl. I have to step out for a moment but I'll be within hearing distance, and I won't be long."

I open my mouth to argue but he places a finger against my lips, then leans down and licks around it. Lust spirals through me. I'm drunk on it.

"No arguing, remember? I promise I won't be long. Just

relax into it. You might be able to come. If you can, you have my permission."

Biting my lip so I don't cuss him out, I watch him leave, praying to all that is holy that he'll be true to his word and come right back.

The rumbling hum against my clit peaks again, and I feel myself gush a little.

There's no way I can get over the edge like this, not with the constant stops and starts, so I distract myself by letting my mind wander.

If only I'd paid more attention to all the BDSM romance novels I devoured back home. Maybe then I'd have a better understanding of why I react this way to his ruthless dominance, his crooned threats, his statements of ownership. And why I always end up being helplessly aroused and indignant at the same time.

He may have a wall up most of the time, but Krav sure knows how to wrap me around his giant, taloned finger when it comes to sex. And surely that's a good start. Plenty of people start out as fuck buddies and wind up being more. I'll figure out a way to reach his heart.

As the vibrations ebb and flow against my thrumming clit, I close my eyes and distract myself from the gnawing ache with a question:

How do you get an emotionally unavailable demon to fall for you, anyway?

NINE

Krav

I DO NOT INTEND to torment my fiery Omega for long but I need a moment to myself, to untangle my thoughts. For as much as I enjoy indulging myself with her physically, she brings unending confusion into my life. Everything was straightforward, predictable... *simple*... before she came along.

And now?

Now my moods shift like the purple sands of the Yazebii desert just beyond my kingdom when the scorching winds twirl them to and fro. Contentment, lust, rage, frustration, and dread seize me without warning, often battling each other for dominance within me.

Mount Vracor is quiet, which proves the myth of it being a reflection of the king's mood to be false. I am in turmoil.

All because of that infuriating, beautiful Hoo-man with hair like flames and a scent more potent than all the *kasewl* in the world. And she had the temerity to accuse me of shutting her out? Of placing some invisible barrier between us so she cannot get close to me? Pah!

I prowl back and forth in the adjacent room to hers, close enough that I can hear her should she call for me but far enough away to have space to think. To regain control.

Did I misjudge our cycles? Am I still in rut? Is that why I feel so… disordered?

Replaying all our recent conversations in my mind, I work to find the source of my current disquiet. Frankly, it could be any or all of them. Renee has a way of riling me unlike anyone I've met before, which is partly why she's now tied to the bed, writhing with frustration, waiting for me to return and grant her what she so desperately wants. I had to reestablish dominance. She is the pet. I am the Master.

Ulf knows, Plutus gives me no such trouble, and he is by far the deadlier of the two.

After the conversation we had about what she referred to as *BDSM*, I thought giving her a collar would be a good way to remind her of her place. I wasn't prepared for the surge of pride I'd feel upon seeing it locked around her pale throat. A symbol of my ownership of her.

My castle is filled with treasures. I've always collected things of beauty, or value, or both, since I was young. I'm also insanely possessive. My mother once remarked on that, after she accidentally spilled some juice on one of my scrolls, ruining it. I flew into such a rage that I almost attacked her. She later confided in me that for a brief moment, she'd been afraid for her life as I ranted and raved, destroying the ruined scroll and several others, shredding them and announcing that she would be next if she touched any of my things again.

It wasn't that she'd ruined the scroll that infuriated me— it was that she'd touched it. "It may be a blessing after all that there are no more Omegas," she said later, when I had calmed down somewhat and apologized for roaring at her. "If you're this possessive over a mere scroll, I dread to think how you'd be with a mate when you're in rut."

"I have no need of a mate," I told her, "since I have no

desire for offspring, and prefer my own company." My father would never approve of my refusal to continue his line, but I was old enough to want to defy him.

She gave me a long, assessing look, her unusual eyes searching my face. Then, "You'll change your mind, my son. When you're grown, you'll come to appreciate what a blessing it is to have a companion in life. You are not meant to rule alone. I pray that Ulf in His wisdom blesses you with an Omega, and if not an Omega, another who can rule beside you as a queen."

Unwilling to argue, I remained silent, but inwardly, I had scoffed. And who was proven right in the end? Who now has an Omega and yet still no inclination to make her his queen? Who uses magic to ensure there will be no offspring?

I do.

I signal to a hovering *jynx* to bring me some wine, and resume pacing. My thoughts return to the present. While I have no plans to make Renee my equal, I do not want to share her with anybody. Nor do I want her to leave. After all, who in their right mind would willingly give up their possessions?

But she's a stubborn little thing, and I have no doubt she will continue to pester me about meeting the other Hoo-man Omegas until I either relent, or am driven insane by her persistent clamoring. I tap my teeth with my talon. There must be a solution.

The servant has returned with my wine. I drain it and am about to return to Renee when the *jynx* tells me there's something I should know.

"Well?" I snap when no more is forthcoming. "What is it?"

News of your new pet has reached Altrim. The Wanderer King and his queen are requesting a meeting.

"They can request all they want," I snarl. "I do not answer to Khan. I do not answer to any of the other kings. Or anyone else!"

The *jynx* is about to leave when it hits me: the solution. So easy. So obvious.

"Wait," I command. "Give them this message: we will convene via the orbs tomorrow as the suns set."

The *jynx* bobs and weaves away. I roll my shoulders, already feeling lighter. By tomorrow, my Omega pet will belong to me as completely as if she were part of my own body. She might still be able to leave, but she will never want to. And I will never have to worry about losing her again.

* * *

Renee

This demon's going to be the death of me. The buzzing against my clit makes my arousal rise in an all-consuming wave, only for it to die away when the little torture device stops its wicked vibration. I'm burning up. I rock but can't move far in my bonds. The motion only jostles the butt plug within me, and waves of feverish heat rush through me. I'm drenched, my leaking pussy soaking the sheets.

How long will he leave me like this? I won't survive it much longer.

"Krav," I groan as the torture device cuts out, leaving me teetering on the precipice. My arousal intensifies from simply saying his name. Imagining him here is enough to make me pant, overwhelmed with pleasure. His salty, dark chocolate scent surrounds me. "Master."

"Did you miss me, pet?" He looms over me, huge and fierce with his horns half in shadow. His arms are crossed over his bare chest, but his tail strokes my leg. I shudder at the simple touch.

"Yes. Please. I need you."

His tail taps the tip of the plug, and my core clenches.

"Fuuuuuck…"

"Oh, I intend to." The purple bastard is enjoying this. "Just a little longer."

"No," I gasp, rising off the bed as far as the bonds allow. "Make me come. Please."

"Do you presume to give me orders? Perhaps I should spank you." Splaying a huge paw over my right breast, he pats it as if considering slapping my nipple. I arch into his touch.

"Yes, please, Master. Anything." I'm so desperate for stimulation, I'll take a spanking. Anything to distract myself from the incessant ebb and flow of arousal.

He reaches for the rope at my ankles and his talons come out with a snicking sound. A few slices of his claws and the ropes fall away. Gripping my ankles with his left hand, he yanks my legs up and lets his right come crashing down. He spanks me like that, tied by my wrists and defenseless. He catches the underside of my buttocks again and again, every impact sending a cacophony of sensation rioting through me, pain and pleasure rolled into one. I'm sobbing, begging, writhing in his grip. I need more.

Both of his hands are busy with holding my legs up and spanking me, but somehow the plug is moving in and out of my ass. Is he using his tail? It's pretty dexterous.

When my butt is blazing and I don't think I can take another single slap, he stops and runs a hand over the stinging skin. With a wicked smirk, holding my gaze, he reaches for the plug between my ass cheeks. Slowly, he pushes it in and pulls it out, pausing every time the widest part of the bulb stretches my orifice to the max. Each turn of the screw makes my arousal spiral higher. The tightness builds in my belly.

The vibrations on my clit are building, building... I can't breathe. When the buzzing reaches its crescendo, Krav tugs the plug out of me. I tumble over the edge, my pussy clenching violently. Pleasure crashes through me, tensing every muscle in my body.

Did I just come from the removal of the plug from my ass?

Tiny aftershocks run through me as the savage waves of pleasure ebb away. The evil device on my clit has switched over to a steady, continuous buzz, the vibration agonizing on my over-sensitive nub. I buck and twist, trying to escape the sensation overload.

"Lovely," he murmurs. "But you're a bad girl. Not only did you come without permission, you didn't even ask for it." His dark, rainbow gaze is intent as he watches me writhe, dangling helpless in his hold. "You'll have to be punished. The question is how…"

Something blunt but rigid probes my rear. I clench my buttocks but can't keep the thick length of his tail away from my now-empty hole.

"Oh fuck—"

Krav slides a finger into my mouth to shush me. I clamp my lips around it, sucking greedily as his tail invades my most private hole. It pushes past the tight ring of muscle, easing forward and withdrawing until it can slide further in. *Please,* I beg with my gaze. Every probe of his tail stimulates the deepest, darkest parts of me. The vibrator humming incessantly on my clit intensifies the sensation a thousandfold.

I open my mouth, releasing his finger with a cry. "Please, Master. Please fuck me—"

Krav extends his wings with a snap. They beat the air, refreshing me with a cooling wind, and for a moment he's airborne before he mounts me, covering me with his giant body, surrounding me with his scent. His wings shiver overhead, framing him as he impales my aching, empty pussy. With the tip of his tail still deep in my ass, I feel every ridge, every bump on his amazing cock as he splits me open, filling me, stretching me beyond what should be possible.

The noises I'm making don't sound human as they mingle with his grunts and echo off the walls.

He fucks me into the bed, the force of his flapping wings driving his cock in to the hilt. His tail skewers me, probing my ass deeper. I'm full, so full, impaled on both his dick and tail, writhing, out of my mind. His pelvis is crushing my clit with every thrust, driving me higher and higher…

"Please," I gasp, unable to formulate the rest.

"Come for me," he commands. His canines look longer than usual. They flash white as he snarls, "Come for me… now."

Pleasure erupts from my core, rippling through me, searing me with white hot ecstasy. My body rocks, out of my control. Gravity loses its grip on me and I levitate, the bindings on my wrists and Krav's weight the only things keeping me down. The whole world trembles.

Krav is roaring. The bed and room are rocking, and there's a distant rumble. Was there an earthquake or did the earth move just for me?

I clench my fists, trying to come back down, wishing I could touch my demon. His wings beat above us, creating a mighty wind, but his body shields me from the worst of it. That familiar searing burn shoots through my sex as his knot forms. Seconds later, he's coming, filling me with boiling hot cum. I clench on his cock and it sets off another round of fireworks in my belly.

He rears up, his dark hair flying, his roar reverberating through me. His canines look like fangs, glinting above me, menacing and deadly. Then he snaps his head down.

Something sharp pricks my neck. Is he freaking *biting* me? Pain flashes through me, stealing my breath. Krav's growl has reached a deafening crescendo, making my lower belly twist and my pussy gush around his throbbing cock.

The sharp ache in the tender junction between my shoulder and neck intensifies before the pain morphs into an avalanche of pleasure.

My whole world has been reduced to sensation: the demon's scent, his deep growl, the heat of his body, and my pussy's frantic clenching around his cock as the orgasm overtakes me—and then, everything goes dark.

A CHORUS of angelic voices brings me back. I swim into awareness as the melody wafts over me, sweet and delicate as notes plucked from a harp. The song fades but I can still hear it deep in my heart, playing so softly, my ears cannot hear it.

Every part of my body is pounding—my heart, my clit, the place where I suspect Krav bit me. I want to touch it, soothe it somehow, but I'm afraid. What if it's bad? What if there's blood?

The hum in my chest is like a fainter version of his purr. It soothes me, tamping down my fear.

It's annoying. I reach for the feeling of frustration before it slips away.

Everything is hazy. I turn my head and get a face full of hair. Krav's nuzzling my neck, rubbing his cheek along mine.

Is he cuddling me?

The song inside me surges. Lightness suffuses my limbs.

But then reality intrudes. I try to move and can only groan. My ass is empty, my body sore. I might not be able to move ever again.

"Shhh, sweet pet." He lowers his head and kisses the top of my shoulder. Heat pulses through me, reawakening the mystical music singing through my core. The melody clashes with the wrung-out ache in the rest of my body.

Krav folds up his wings and rolls to his back beside me, a

content smirk on his face. He keeps one huge hand resting on my belly.

A part of me likes his possessiveness. A part of me wants to punch him. "Did you… did you actually *bite* me?"

"Yes." He doesn't sound the least bit sorry.

"Unbelievable!" I say. "I mean, I get that you got carried away, and I know I seem to get off on pain these days, but that freaking hurt!"

"Allow me," he murmurs, leaning down. His breath tickles my shoulder and then his tongue is on me, laving the sore spot. The sharp sting fades instantly.

The humming in my chest resumes. "Thank you."

He caresses my cheek with a long, thick finger. "Do not look so cross, little Omega. Don't you realize what I just did?"

"Of course I do. You tied me to the bed and fucking left me alone! For hours! With that *thing* on me… driving me crazy!"

His chuckle rumbles through me. "Was it not worth it in the end?"

"Not really. I mean, it's not like I have any trouble getting off with you *without* being edged for a million years first."

He snorts. "It wasn't a million years, nor was it even a single hour. You exaggerate, as you so often do."

"I do *not* exaggerate!"

"In any case, that wasn't what I was referring to. I meant the bite. It has significance. Great significance." His hand splays wider over my abdomen, warming me.

"Which would be?" The humming in my chest is weirdly soporific, like Krav's purr. I smother a yawn.

"It's called the claiming bite," he explains, his rainbow topaz eyes gleaming. "When an Alpha and Omega are destined to be mates, the Alpha claims her by giving her that bite. It joins them together… forever. They are now not only lovers; they are soul-bonded."

I'm so exhausted, it takes a moment for his words to fully sink in. "Huh?" I manage.

"You are now mine, Renee. Fully. Completely. As if you were a part of me. We share a bond that can never be broken."

I slump back against the cushions, staring at the ornate ceiling, my mind whirling. The trilling music in my chest has quieted, but it's still there. "But… you already said you own me. Several times. Before… this."

"Of course, and I did. You were mine from the first moment I saw you, tied to that *cex*, your bare flesh glistening in the sunlight…"

"I was there. I remember," I mutter wryly.

"But now you're more than my pet. You're bound to me, for always. The bond runs so deep, it is said that the couple can feel each other's emotions."

"Assuming they have any," I mutter. Then I feel bad. He's opening up to me without any prompting. I should encourage it. "Sorry. I think I'm just tired."

"You're right. We should rest for a while." He settles himself back down, nuzzling my shoulder. Weird how it's become second nature to dodge his horns whenever he puts his head near me.

Is he crazy? I can't sleep now! I have to know: is this weird new melody in my chest something to do with the bond? Why did he decide to do it? Does it have anything to do with the collar he made for me? What's going on? I need him to answer my questions. "So is this bond thing like a marriage?" I ask.

"Marriage?" He stumbles over the English word.

"Back home, it's a ritual we have to bind couples—usually, it's couples—together for life. They exchange vows, rings, their families and friends join them for a big celebration, the bride tends to wear a white dress, there are flowers, a cake…"

"Sounds complicated." Now it's Krav's turn to yawn. I

peek at him while he does so, admiring his pointed canines and long, long tongue.

"It can be complicated, if you make it so. But the point is that the people who are in love are then considered joined together for life. Forever." Should I bother explaining divorce? He doesn't know about Phillip yet—or much about my life in Houston at all. He never asks about my past.

"Then yes, I would say it is similar. And much simpler. Your wound will heal, although your shoulder will bear the mark forever."

"You freaking *scarred* me?" I move to sit up, hot outrage washing over me, but then the fucker begins to purr, and his rumble joins the hum in my own chest. It's like being shot up with a million ccs of valium. My body grows heavy. Calm. At ease. "Don't pull that sneaky little trick on me now, Krav, we need to talk about this!"

The hand not on my belly finds my hair and strokes the top of my head, melting me the way it always does. "Hush, sweet thing." His words are like crashing waves I can't battle. "What's done is done. You're mine—my pet, my Omega, my gift. Surely you've realized by now that I can do whatever I like with you. What's more, you enjoy it. Whether you admit it, or squeak in feigned outrage."

Do I? His words suffuse me with warmth, a non-sexual heat which envelops my chest. Or maybe it's just my first hot flash. Is forty-one too young to start having those? Christ, I hope so. I sure miss being able to look stuff like that up. Hell, I miss my phone, period.

"The urge to claim you that way has been getting stronger every day," Krav admits. He's still purring, jumbling my thoughts, wrapping me in an enthralling cocoon of safety. Contentment. Affection.

"Has it?" My eyelids are drooping even as my heart skips with hope. Does this mean my feelings for him are mutual? Maybe it's because he's purring at the same time, but his speech is slurred. Drowsy. Like he's had a bit too much wine and is oversharing. Is this the alien equivalent of *in vino, veritas*—confessing your true feelings because you're drunk?

"Of course. I'm extremely possessive, even my mother said so. And now that I've claimed you, you're safe from other Alphas. No one else can have you. Everyone will know you belong to me."

He presses a kiss to my shoulder, and I would shiver if I could summon the energy to move.

"It was the message I got from Khan requesting a meeting that made me decide," he goes on. "If we're soul-bonded, you won't want to leave…"

He trails off into a light snore while I stare at the ceiling with wide, stunned eyes, feeling like I just got doused with ice-water. "Message from Khan?" I squeak, trying desperately to place the name. I'm sure he's mentioned it before. "Who's Khan? Krav! What meeting? Master! Oh, hell no!"

How the heck is he still purring while he's asleep? Summoning all my energy, fighting the paralyzing sense of relaxation, I roll over to face him, shoving at his shoulder.

"Wake up!" Jesus, he weighs a freaking ton. The wall of muscle that makes up his torso doesn't shift the slightest bit beneath my hands. "You can't fall asleep now! Wake up, goddammit! I have *questions*!" My voice is ringing in my ears, joining the cacophony of rumbling purr and soft, rhythmic snores. It matches the hum deep in my chest, inside my heart.

The sheet barely covers his groin. A well-placed tweak would almost certainly wake him up, but then he'd either be horny, or pissed. And I don't want either of those outcomes right now. I want answers.

"Okay," I say through clenched teeth. "I get it. You're tired." I roll back over until I'm once again staring at the ceiling, willing myself to take deep breaths. "I'll let you get some shuteye. But you can't sleep forever. And when you wake up… you'd better be giving me some answers, big boy."

For a long time, I lie awake, running an entire gamut of emotions as his casually dropped statements replay through my mind. His dark rasp echoes in my ears... *Bond that can never be broken... destined to be mates... part of me... together forever... more than my pet...*

Maybe I was wrong about him. He is a demon, after all—and an alien one at that—I can't expect him to behave like a regular human guy. And it's not like I've met any other Ulfarri Alphas or kings to compare. Maybe they all act that way. Maybe treating their partners more like pampered fuck buddies than equals is typical Ulfarri behavior.

I sigh, tracing my collar with a fingertip. Gift giving *is* one of the five love languages. Back home, there are people who love their pets more than they love their spouse. He does try so hard to please me, give me everything I want… and from what I understand, now he's done the Ulfarri equivalent of making me his wife.

That certainly isn't fuckboi behavior.

It's love.

A smile spreads over my face. Sure, he's a demon, we're on a different planet with no coffee or internet, and so far, I seem to spend most of my time here either in a sexual frenzy, or confused as heck. But I sure as hell didn't have any luck with guys on Earth—and none of them ever came close to being as good in bed as Krav. Not to mention, he can do magic and has a pet griffin. And when he looks at me a certain way and strokes my cheek, I freaking *worship* him.

Lulled by his gentle purrs, soothed by his protective hand on my belly, I close my eyes at last and let the darkness wash over me.

If we're soul-bonded, you won't want to leave…

If that ain't a declaration of feelings, I don't know what is.

TEN

Krav

I OPEN my eyes to see Renee peering down at me. Her hair tumbles over her bare shoulders, the morning sunlight bringing out the hidden glints of gold in the red tresses. Each strand shimmers like a fire-stone—both golden and crimson tones undulating like a flame. A fitting color for a demon's pet.

"Bout time you woke up," she says. The air is redolent with her tantalizing, musky *talliox* scent.

"Did you sleep at all?" I must have been exhausted to have fallen asleep beside her and stayed there. Even after we rut, I'm careful to return to my own bed.

"I did. Eventually. After I spent a good while cursing you for passing out on me when you did. Talk about a cliffhanger!"

I blink, confused as I so often am when she speaks. "A what?"

"Khan," she says, drawing out his name. A flash of irritation sparks through me at another's name on her lips. Strange.

"You said you got a message from Khan requesting a meeting. Who is he?"

"The Wanderer King," I say, yawning and pulling myself up to a semi-sitting position. "Word of your appearance here has reached other kingdoms. The Pyredii are slow to gossip, but they still do it. Khan and his queen asked to talk to me."

"His… *human* queen?"

I can sense her excitement through the bond like a joyful melody, and it pleases me. "Yes, sweetheart, his Hoo-man Omega."

"When are you having this meeting? I assume I'm invited too?"

For the briefest instant, I consider lying to her and calling everything off. Then she turns her head, revealing the mark that ties her to me to the exclusion of all others. The tightness in my chest eases. "Tonight, when the suns set. And yes, you will be there."

Renee squeals and claps her hands. "Yay! Ohmigosh, this is just the best thing ever!" Then, seeing my face, "Well, not the best thing *ever*, obviously… it's just an Earth saying, okay?" She gives me a hurried kiss then scrambles out of the bed. Her naked body tempts me to drag her back to me but she's already tugging on her gown. "I need a shower. I need to decide what to wear. I have so many questions for the queen. What's her name?"

"I will make you something to wear," I tell her immediately. There's no way I would allow Khan to see her in such a transparent gown. "And her name is…" I cast my mind back to that council meeting so many moons ago, "*Emma*, I believe."

"Emma! Emma, Emma, Emma…" Renee is giddy. Warmth spreads through my chest, surprising me. I knew I would be able to sense the Omega's emotions through the bond but never imagined it would feel quite so vivid.

"Do not forget who owns you, pet," I remind her. "The

meeting will only take place if you agree to do and wear what I say."

Renee cocks her head, her hands sliding to her hips as they always do when she's in a defiant mood. "How d'you mean? You gonna make me go naked?"

I bark out a laugh. "Of course not. The very idea is preposterous."

"Well then. Shoot, I'd probably agree to wear a dang chicken costume if it means I get to hang out with someone in the same boat as me."

"Chicken?"

"A kind of bird back home. Extremely popular food source."

"Ah."

"Do they have far to come?"

"To come?" It takes a moment for me to understand. "Oh, no, they're not traveling here. We're meeting via the orbs."

Her shoulders sag. "Oh." Then, as is typical for her, she brightens. "Never mind. At least I'll get to talk to her. She will be able to hear me, right?"

"Of course."

"And see me?"

"Yes."

"Excellent! I need to get a shower." She turns to leave and my gaze wanders—as it always does—to the plump curves of her ass. As if she can feel my eyes on her, she holds up a hand, still walking to the door. "Don't even *think* about joining me. I haven't forgotten last time. And I need to get clean, not filthier. You can either wait, or avail yourself of one of the other facilities."

I grin at her sass but keep my voice stern. "Are you giving me orders, little Omega?"

"Just this once. Don't worry, I'll atone for it later." With that, she vanishes from my sight.

I stretch my stiff muscles, clamber out of the bed and set

off for my own bathroom, already picturing the dress I will make for her.

By the time she joins me in the great room, the garment is finished. "Here," I say, handing it to her. "For this evening."

"Thank you!" She holds it up, turning it this way and that. "Gorgeous fabric. It changes color with the light! Now it's green… and now it looks blue!"

"Just like your eyes," I tell her. "Want to try it on now? In case I need to make any adjustments."

"You never need to make any adjustments but I'll try it on anyhow." Tugging off the dress she put on after her shower, she pulls the new gown over her head. "Ow. The bite mark is still sore." But there's a smug little hum in the bond. Part of her likes the pain.

My adorable, submissive Omega. "It should heal completely soon," I say. "In the meantime, tell me whenever it gets sore and I'll make it better."

"Just a sec." She draws the hem down over her round hips and it drops to the floor. "Wow."

"Don't you like it?" I'm struggling to read her expression.

"No, I do, I love it! I just don't think I've felt so… dressed… since I first arrived here! You can't see through this material at all. It's even got long sleeves!"

"The cold season is upon us," I say. "Look."

Her gaze follows the direction of my outstretched arm until she sees the thick flakes tumbling from the sky. "Is that… snow?" She rushes over to the window, almost tripping over the hem of her new dress. "Holy crap, that's pretty. It's *purple*!"

"The sand from a nearby desert gets caught in the wind and mixes with the flakes, giving it that color," I tell her, leaning back in my chair.

"It's white where I come from. Although it hardly ever snows in Texas. I never would've thought it would snow here."

"It hasn't for many years. The last time was when my mother was alive."

She wrinkles her nose. "You don't have regular seasons?"

I shrug. "We have fires in the summer and deep freeze in the winter."

"So it's either ice cold or burning lava hot," Renee says, returning to stand before me.

"Yes." I reach out and capture her hands. They're always cold. I plant them on my chest and let my heart-fire heat her through.

"At least the snow's pretty. Shame it dissolves in the lava."

When her hands have regained enough warmth, she slides them up my chest and hugs my neck. "Thank you," she murmurs. "For arranging the meeting."

I turn my head and lick the bite mark to make it stop hurting. Renee shivers.

"That feels so much better, thank you." To my amazement, she settles herself in my lap. "Not gonna lie, I was pretty mad last night when you dropped all that stuff on me and conked out. But you stayed with me until morning, purring until I fell asleep, keeping your arm around me—and now, making me this lovely dress, letting me meet Emma—"

"What's *Christmas*?" I interrupt. I need to change the course of this conversation before she asks more about why I spent the whole night beside her. "You mentioned it the last time we talked about snow."

"Oh. It's this thing we have back home every year in winter. People put trees in their homes and decorate them with brightly colored lights and baubles and tinsel."

"Tinsel?"

"Shiny, metallic stuff, usually gold or silver. Like thread? It glitters. It's a type of decoration. The whole holiday is about bringing light to a dark time. About coming together and sharing warmth in the middle of a harsh winter. Spreading holiday cheer. People send each other cards, and give each other gifts. On the night before Christmas, they leave cookies and milk out for Santa, who comes down the chimney while everyone's asleep and puts gifts under the tree for the kids."

"Santa?"

"A jolly figure with a big white beard who wears a red suit and hat trimmed with fur, and lives in the North Pole with his elves."

"How does Santa know what gifts to bring?"

"Kids either write him a list, or their parents take them to the mall. There, they sit in his lap—" she wriggles in mine, playing with the braids of my own beard, "—and tell him what they want. If they were good all year, he grants their wish."

I raise an eyebrow. "Only if they were good? And how would he know?"

"Because he's not real. Their parents pretend he is. They're the ones who get the gifts and put them under the tree while the kids are asleep, then say it was Santa. Just like the parents are the ones who hide the eggs at Easter instead of the Easter Bunny, and put money under kids' pillows instead of the Tooth Fairy…"

"Easter Bunny? Tooth Fairy? What are they?"

Renee explains and I listen to her excited chatter, the warmth in my chest spreading with her obvious joy. Her cheeks are flushed, her eyes sparkling. I've never seen her so animated.

It occurs to me that her happiness is entirely due to the prospect of talking to the other Hoo-man. It has nothing to do with me. Since she got here, I've done everything in my power to put such a broad smile on her face, but nothing I did delighted her this much.

The thought is like a dagger in my gut.

"…so then they put their baby tooth under their pillow, and the Tooth Fairy—in other words, their *parents*, as per usual—replaces the tooth with money. Krav? Are you still listening? You look like you're miles away."

"I'm listening. Money. Pillow." Ulf only knows what a *fairy* is but I have no desire to find out.

"Good." She snuggles against me, her hand splayed over my chest. "Anyway, enough talk of human customs. I just wanted to say thank you for making this the best day ever. For letting me talk to Emma."

I press a kiss to the top of her head. "I just hope she's able to answer your questions, pet." *And I hope you ask the right questions.* Despite the claiming bite, I'm still nervous that Renee will discover it's possible to return to Earth—and want to go. That's the problem with live possessions. You cannot control them completely.

"I'm sure she will. After all, she'll understand what it feels like… to be on a different planet, to be turned into an Omega, to be claimed by an Alpha king." She tenses. "Wait, she did get claimed by him, right? They have that same bond thing we do?"

"The soul-bond. Yes." Khan would never have risked bringing Emma into a room with several other Alphas if he hadn't claimed her, binding her to him first.

She relaxes in my arms. "Good. Then she'll know."

"Know what?"

"Everything, I hope. I have so many questions."

"Indeed you do." I reach into my pocket and bring out the other gift I made for her along with the dress. "Here," I say, laying it across her thighs. "For you."

"Seriously?" She picks up the shimmering pink leash, rubbing her fingers over it. "Is this what I think it is?"

"To clip to your collar." I force my tone to remain jovial. "Can't have you running away."

"It's pretty. I guess there's no harm in wearing it. I did promise to wear what you asked me."

"You did. You're a good girl."

For the first time, I can physically feel her reaction to my praise. A warm glow suffuses her, and the bond between us hums a pleasant melody. "Thank you."

"*My* good girl." I hold her tight for a moment before releasing her reluctantly. "Now, as much as I'd like to sit here all day, I need to get things ready for the call."

As if in response, Renee's belly growls. I chuckle.

"And we should have some food." I signal the *jynx*.

"Okay." My pet clambers off my lap. "I do have one request of my own, though."

"What is it?"

"No more of that goddamn horny tea, please!" She rolls her eyes but she's smiling.

"The *kasewl*?"

"Yeah. I do not want to be all riled up and panting with lust while I'm talking to Emma. I promise you can do anything you want to me afterwards."

"I know. And I will." Getting to my feet, I slide a hand to cup her neck and draw her to me, bending to speak directly in her ear. "And don't pretend it was the *kasewl* that made your little cunt all hot and achy for me. *I* do that to you. It's the way you always react to me. You know why?"

A gasp slipped out of her while I was speaking, and I'm gratified by the sudden change in her demeanor. "Why?"

"Because you were *made* for me."

ELEVEN

Renee

At last the suns are setting and I'm about to meet Emma. I can't remember the last time a day dragged the way this one did.

Krav is on edge. God knows why. What does he think they're gonna do, whisk me away through the orb? Then again, I guess this *is* Ulfaria. Anything is possible.

He clipped the leash to my collar before we sat down and now he's gripping the other end in a tight fist. I've heard of possessive guys but this is a whole new level.

Still, I can't deny that I find all this ownership stuff a bit thrilling. Throughout our marriage, but especially towards the end, Phillip didn't care at all where I was or what I was doing. What is it they say? The opposite of love isn't hate, it's indifference.

The orb is floating in front of us, and it's much smaller than I imagined. I hope I can see Emma clearly. Despite what Krav might think, I'm not real fussed about Khan. Sure, it'll be interesting to observe another Alpha king, but I'm not nearly as curious about him as I am about the other human who's also been through this whole crazy experience.

There's a flicker on the smooth surface, and slowly two bodies come into focus. One is huge, hulking, lilac-skinned, with long hair and a beard. He looks like a freaking pirate. The other is much smaller—and human—with blonde hair, and skin almost as pale as mine. "Emma!" I squeal. "So nice to meet you!"

"Hi!" she says, "Great to see you too!" Her accent sounds faintly British.

It's so good to hear someone speak my own language, to see someone who looks familiar even though we've never met before. I bite my lip, overcome with emotion.

"Thank you for granting us this audience," Khan says rather formally. I suddenly wish the guys weren't here and I could talk to Emma alone. Next time, maybe. Once Krav sees there's no harm in it.

"Renee was keen to speak to your Omega," Krav says, laying a possessive hand on my thigh. He's still clutching my leash with the other. "And I cannot deny my pet anything."

I resist the urge to roll my eyes.

"But I must ask that you Hoo-mans speak our language," Khan says. "Please."

"Of course. Sorry," I say, feeling sheepish. "I didn't mean to be rude."

"Don't worry," Emma says, "We'll just have to chat again another time… alone." She shoots a pointed look at the hulking demon beside me. "The other girls and I try to get together when we can—it's a great way to let off steam and compare notes. You could join us."

"I'd love that!" I mean it. A woman cannot live on sex alone. She also needs gal pals.

Emma's eyes widen as she clocks the collar around my neck, and the leash leading to Krav's taloned fist. She glances up at her Alpha with a knowing smile before addressing me. "Nice collar. You into BDSM?"

"I always suspected I might be," I confess, "but it wasn't until I got here that… well… let's just say a whole new side of me has been unleashed. No pun intended."

Emma giggles. "It's wild, isn't it? This Omega thing? The way you crave everything they do to you?"

"It is." My cheeks are warm. Damn Krav for claiming me like a pet, and damn my pussy for thinking it's hot. I clear my throat. "How many other queens—human women—are there?"

"With you, there's five of us, now," Emma says, and warmth spears my chest at the inclusion. "That we know of. So far. People are still looking in case more were brought over but," she shrugs, "Ulfaria is a big place. Nine known kingdoms, not including a great chunk where no one ever ventures. The Wastelands. God only knows what goes on over there."

"How long have you been here? How did you get here? How are you surviving without chocolate?" Excitement makes me babble.

"I've been here a while," Emma says. "Long enough to start a family."

"Holy shit!"

She laughs. "Yeah. Emilia, and now Kharon. Our little angels. They're just… the best. It's weird, I never wanted kids, but now I can't imagine my life without them."

There's a pang in my chest. "I did want them, but it just never seemed to be the right time while I was married. Then I got divorced, and though I've dated since then, there wasn't anybody serious. Now I'm forty-one, so I kinda made peace with the idea that it just won't happen for me." Krav shifts beside me and I risk a glance at him. But if hearing about my ex-husband bothers him, he's not outwardly showing it.

"That's not too old!" Emma says. "Plenty of women have kids in their forties."

"Yeah… I mean, the playground's still open, so to speak, but with every year, fertility decreases and risks increase. Not to mention the time it would still take to find someone suitable, and willing, and *committed*…"

Emma shoots a knowing glance at Krav, rigid beside me. "In my experience, Ulfarri Alphas are all about the breeding. That's basically the whole point of their desperation to find Omegas. Isn't that right, my love?" She pats Khan's hand. "You were so keen to knock me up, you kept trying even *after* I got pregnant!"

I chuckle.

"Omegas are known for their fertility," Emma says. "Not sure how that affects human biology—whether it would mean a less risky pregnancy for you or whatever—but you could talk to the magicians about it. They might know."

"Magicians?" I ask.

She waves an airy hand. "Back home, we'd call them scientists."

"Right. Maybe I will." I want to, if Krav will allow it. It took him long enough to agree for me to meet Emma, but he granted my request in the end. I glance at him. He's back to doing a gargoyle impression, rigid and unmoving beside me.

Emma is still talking. "As to how I got here… it's a long story. The short version is: I was abducted by aliens—a different species to Ulfarri, they're known as Ogsul—and Khan rescued me from the auction block. Out of the frying pan…"

"…into the alien fire," I finish for her. "Did the other women get here the same way?"

Emma shakes her head. "The Ogsul created this serum—the stuff that turns us regular lil humans into compatible Omegas. King Aurus wanted heirs, so he commissioned the

Ogsul to find more of us and bring at least one here for him. The Stone King got wind of it, and decided he wanted a slice of that pie. God knows how many he had the Ogsul deliver before he met his well-deserved demise."

I shake my head. "Ordering us like we're pizzas. It's disgusting."

"I know. Don't get me wrong, I'm deliriously happy now, but it was a rough start. I almost went home when I got the chance," Emma says.

Out of nowhere, a chill spreads through my whole body even as a surge of hope fills my chest—like I don't know how to feel about Emma's revelation. "You found a way to go home?" I squeak.

Krav's hand tightens on my thigh, the tips of his claws digging menacingly into my flesh through the gown. A not-so-subtle warning.

"Yes! Aurus has a team of eggheads—his magicians—who managed to find a way. Not entirely without risk, but possible. But when it came down to it…" she glances at Khan with a look of such devotion, it makes me ache, "I couldn't leave him."

"Awww. I'm a sucker for a romantic story," I admit.

"That's why we asked to see you," Emma goes on. "The Ulfarri are known across the galaxy as the Brutal Ones. Just because I got lucky—and the other women so far—well, let's just say not all the kings are good, or kind. The Stone King, for instance, was just…" She trails off with a shudder. "When we heard you had turned up here, we wanted to make sure you were okay. Cause if you want to go home, we can arrange it."

A low, threatening growl bursts out of Krav's chest and I grip the arms of my chair, my head spinning. I had low-key hoped that leaving would be an option, but it was the same kind of hope you have when you buy a lottery ticket. Not

impossible, but improbable. Now, to hear it's a possibility…
that has to sink in.

"My pet has no desire to leave." Krav's voice is like
thunder. "She's happy here, with me. I have claimed her. I
own her."

Emma shifts her cool blue gaze to the demon beside me.
"Respectfully, we're asking her, not you."

"I *am* happy," I say hastily. Anything to diffuse the sudden
tension. "Like you, I had a bumpy start, but…" I trail off,
trying to corral my whirling thoughts. "And anyway, he's
claimed me now. Doesn't that mean I can no longer leave?"

Khan scoffs. "You can still leave. The bond would ache—
for both of you—but if he told you otherwise, he was lying."

"He said I *won't want to* leave," I correct myself. I get the
sense Krav is one wrong word away from ending this
meeting, and I'm not ready for that. "My bad. He did explain
it. Us being soul-bonded. The claiming bite being kinda like
a marriage. He never told me I can't leave."

Khan's piercing stare is fixed on Krav, who has puffed out
his chest and is vibrating with outrage beside me. "Good."

I squeeze Krav's hand, still clenched painfully on my
thigh. "Krav does everything in his power to make me
happy," I tell the couple reflected in the orb. "And like I said,
we had a bit of a bumpy start but then things got a whole lot
better." I want to de-escalate the situation but as I speak, a
glowing ember of doubt starts to fizz in my gut. Things got a
whole lot better last night, after he claimed me. If I take off
my rose-colored glasses, I do have to admit that it's still way
too early to tell for certain. New relationship energy is a
thing.

"If you're sure," Emma says, shooting Krav some almost
imperceptible side-eye before directing her gaze back to me.
"If you change your mind, let us know."

"How?"

"Krav will tell us," Khan says. "After all, he's declared his intentions to see you happy. If going back to Earth was what you wanted, surely he would help you."

I open my mouth to reply but Krav is quicker. "I dislike your tone!" he bellows, leaning forward like he's about to jump into the orb and throttle Khan. "You have no authority over me, and the only reason I agreed to this… this…" he waves a hand, "conversation was to please my Omega! I will not be insulted in my own home!"

Emma remains impressively calm in the face of Krav's spitting fury. "Then we all want the same thing," she says coolly. "For Renee to be happy."

Krav has backed himself into a corner. To argue now would be to admit that Khan and Emma's assumptions are wrong and he wouldn't help me contact them if I wanted to leave. No doubt they said what they did on purpose to test him. And it worked. "Indeed," he says at length, leaning back in his chair. Despite his forced display of ease, he's squeezing my thigh as tightly as ever. "My pet only needs to tell me what she wants, and I will grant it."

Emma glances at Khan, whose face remains impassive. If Krav's sudden display of aggression rattled him, he's not showing it. "I thought as much," the blonde says. "Sorry if we offended you. I'm just so livid at the whole situation… human women being kidnapped and brought over here… I couldn't do anything to stop it, but I am doing what I can to make sure we find them, and help them. I'm sure you understand."

Personally, I'm not so sure he does at all but Krav nods.

"How are we speaking their language?" I ask, desperate to change the subject.

"The Ogsul implanted chips in us, I'm afraid," Emma says, tapping a spot just below her ear. "If you press against the skin here, you might be able to feel it."

"Ugh. Nah, I'm good, thanks," I say. "Guess it's done now. And at least we can communicate."

"Yeah. As scary as it all is, especially at first, it'd be so much worse if you couldn't understand anything or speak to anyone."

I suppress a shudder. "True."

"And between you and me, I would hate to miss out on this one's brand of dirty talk. He has that *down!*" Emma says in English before giving Khan an apologetic smile.

"He's not the only one!" I reply, also in English.

"Enough!" Krav booms. "As you can see, my pet is well taken care of. And now we must go. Kingdom to rule, villagers to terrorize, you know how it is. Lots to do." He hasn't gotten out of his seat, but if this were a dinner party back home, he'd be handing Khan and Emma their keys and herding them towards the door.

It's on the tip of my tongue to argue, to ask what the hell we have to do that's so important, but his mood is volatile and I don't want to push my luck. Nor do I want to give him an excuse to refuse if—make that *when*—I ask to speak to Emma again. So I put on a big smile and give her a little wave. "Lovely talking to you," I say. "I have plenty more questions but I guess they'll have to wait."

"Are you sure you can't stay on a bit longer?" she asks, twin lines of concern appearing between her eyebrows.

To hide my disappointment at things ending so abruptly, I indicate my collar. "Gotta do what the Big Boss says," I say lightly. "We can talk another time. Let me know when the next girls' night is planned."

Emma is staring at me. Her gaze flicks to my neck, the leash Krav is still holding, and back to my face. "As long as it's consensual," she says slowly. "Don't forget that."

"Well, obviously winding up here in the first place wasn't exactly a choice," I say, "but Krav and I have certainly had conversations about consent. Haven't we, Master?" I use the term intentionally, gratified when his massive shoulders relax slightly.

"We have." His voice is even gruffer than usual. "Have a pleasant evening," he tells Khan and Emma briskly. Before they can respond, he waves a hand, and the orb goes dark.

Resisting the urge to go off on him for being so rude to them and cutting our call short, I hold my breath, waiting for the explosion I'm sure is coming.

Instead, his grip on my thigh relaxes. When I look over, I'm struck by how his shoulders sag, how defeated he looks. My heart goes out to him.

"Thank you for that," I say at length, stroking his fingers. "I'm sorry if you felt excluded when we spoke English. It was just… I never realized how good, how *familiar* it would feel to hear my native tongue again."

"I understand," he says.

I'm not sure I believe him but I go to him regardless. I don't know where this urge to comfort him is coming from, especially given the way he just behaved, but something in me senses he's reacting out of fear, and so kicking up a stink right now would be pouring fuel onto the fire. Another thing I learned in therapy.

"Pet," he mutters as I clamber into his lap.

"Master," I whisper, snuggling against his too-warm chest, breathing him in. A spark of joy thrums along the bond we now share.

"You are happy, are you not?" His hesitant tone is so out of character with his usual cocky self-assurance.

"I am," I tell him. "I had the best day today."

More tension seeps out of him. "Good."

As we cuddle silently in the warm glow of the floating orbs they use here instead of light bulbs, I refuse to dwell on the ember of doubt still glowing deep in my gut. Instead, I concentrate on a single thought: Krav behaves this way because he's terrified of losing me. Which can only mean he cares about me. Sure, he's not great at showing it—yet—but he can learn. More cracks in that invisible wall he has around his heart are appearing every day.

And since I've apparently fallen for him hook, line, and sinker, the onus is on me to knock the rest of that sucker down.

I always did enjoy a challenge.

TWELVE

My pet bounds into the dining hall early the next morning and skids to a halt. "What's that sound?"

I was humming a tune my mother used to play, a common melody beloved by her home village.

Renee cocks her head. "You were singing."

"I was not." I try to look fierce and hope she doesn't notice how, though I am silent, the tune plays on in our bond.

"It sounds like a song back on Earth. A Christmas song. *Let it snow,*" she trills.

"It is definitely not an Earth song."

"I know that." She rolls her eyes. "Anyway. I have an idea for today." When I arch an eyebrow, waiting for her to continue, she claps her hands. "Let's go on an adventure!"

She's so adorable, prancing around the table. I toss the scroll I was holding—unread—onto the nearby pile. "Where do you wish to go?"

"Could we leave the castle?"

I stiffen, my wings quivering. Is this how it begins? Is she trying to leave? I rub my chest. No. She said *we*. My tail snakes out to circle her ankle and draw her close, tugging gently so she doesn't trip. She lets me guide her into my lap.

"Not for long. Just for a little while." She plants her hands on my chest to relieve their chill. I cover them with one of mine.

"It's not safe." This morning her scent is light and soft as the snow that's been falling. My body thrums with arousal, desire pulsing through my core.

"I'd be safe with you." She relaxes against me, freeing a hand to toy with the beads in my beard. "Just a quick flight? I'll be good." She bites her lower lip and glances up at me from beneath her long lashes. "It'd be nice to get some fresh air."

The dining hall windows frame Mount Vracor. I will it to smoke or spew lava, but it remains silent. "Very well."

"Yay!" Renee slides out of my lap and does a little dance. Her breasts jiggle seductively beneath her flimsy gown. I watch her hungrily for a few moments before drawing her back.

"You will do as I say at all times." My tail squeezes her leg. "You will remain still, and hold tight to me during our flight —do not let go, no matter what happens. Any deviation from those rules will be punished."

"I understand," she says. I raise a brow and she tacks on a hasty, "Master."

I run a hand over her ass. "Then I agree to this outing. But later... once we return... you will spend the rest of the day showing your gratitude to me."

Ulf, I adore the way her eyes darken when I command her. "How do you propose I do that?" Her voice is husky.

"I'm sure I'll think of something. Several things. Depends on whether you behave. Are you going to be a good girl for me?"

She nods. Pressing her delectable body against mine, she

reaches up and takes hold of the base of my right horn, sending a shiver through me. Her fingers are so small, they don't reach all the way around. "Yes, Master. I'm always a good girl." She lets out a little chuckle.

Her laughter is infectious and I can't suppress a grin. "Unless you want to be spanked," I counter in a low voice. "Then you're more of a naughty one."

Her green eyes are glittering as she gazes at me. "Maybe so. But you love it."

"I do. Sometimes. On this occasion, however, I mean what I say: it's very important that you obey the rules I set out. Am I clear? It's for your safety."

Renee presses a kiss to my cheek. There's a delighted hum in the bond. "I understand," she says. "I promise."

"That's my good girl."

Less than an hour later, we're standing on the ramparts of the second highest tower, overlooking the lava lake. The suns are out but the wind is fierce, buffeting the castle with gusts that would knock over a lesser being.

I keep my arms around Renee, my wings surrounding us like a shield. This part of the turret was specially designed for taking flight. There are no walls or crenellations to get in my way. Nothing to stop my pet from being blown over the edge.

"Ready?" I shout against the wind. She nods against my chest. I scoop her up and she threads her arms around my neck, as I ordered her to. She's a snug bundle, wrapped up in the thick fur robes I conjured for her. There's no way she can fall—I would never drop her—but I want her to cling to me all the same.

Her breath catches as I step to the edge. Instead of running to launch, I give a lazy leap and let my wings billow out as gravity pulls us down. We drift a moment before I catch the fine current that streams between the two lesser towers of my castle. I built the extra turret for this exact purpose—to channel the wind underneath this platform and make it easy for me to soar. My father would have scoffed and accused me of laziness, but it's an easier and more enjoyable start to a flight.

From the way Renee giggles in my arms, she thinks it's fun, too.

I let the current carry us toward Mount Vracor. A short while ago, smoke would have shrouded its peak, but the air is clearer lately. The snow settled the ash.

I flap my wings, gaining height. I would fly up to the summit, but the air is thinner there, and any lingering smoke might harm my pet's lungs. Besides, it would take too long. This outing should be short. The heavy, low-hanging clouds on the horizon portend more snow. As much as my pet loves snow and the way it reminds her of her Hoo-man holiday, she chills easily.

Renee is very still in my arms. "Breathe, sweetheart," I command and nuzzle her hair.

She exhales in a rush.

Once we're as high as I want to be, I stretch out my wings. We soar past the volcano, looping towards the castle and back again in a lazy spiral. "Is this what you wanted?"

"Yes." Her voice is faint in the whistling wind. "It's beautiful."

I chuckle. "There aren't many who would agree with you." Pyreda, land of smoke and lava, birthplace of life, ruled by demons.

"You don't think it's beautiful?" She sounds indignant.

I'm silent for a while, thinking. Beneath us, our combined shadow glides over the barren and wasted land. Soon the ground will freeze enough for the snow to settle. But in the lake of fire, the lava will still burn.

"It is beautiful, in its own way. Fiery red on top with orange markings. A touch of green. Unpredictable and fiery, especially at night." I clutch Renee tighter. She wrinkles her nose and I add, "Wet in its most secret places—"

My pet frees an arm to thump my shoulder. "I meant Pyreda, not me."

I snarl and she hastily wraps her arm back around my neck. I make a mental note to punish her later for disobeying my mandate. "It is said the king and the land are one and the same," I tell her.

"That may be, but I'm not the king."

"You are soul-bonded to me, are you not? Close your eyes. You might be able to feel it."

Her whole face scrunches as she concentrates.

"Can you sense the fires at the heart of the kingdom? The borders?"

"No." She opens her eyes. "Can you?"

"Yes. If I really want to." If I still my mind, I can sense the slow, ancient heartbeat. "My powers weaken if I fly beyond the borders."

"Really?"

I nod. It is one of the reasons why my father never tried to conquer other kingdoms. Even if he'd built a powerful army, he would have had to rely on and trust others— lieutenants—to rule them. Which he would never have done. He never trusted anyone.

Our flight path is taking us over the lake of lava. Even though there's no chance of my dropping Renee, I grip her tighter. Aside from the day she first arrived, I haven't carried anyone this way since I became king and continued my father's tradition of terrorizing the village leaders. Back then, I snatched up a few of the most insistent ones and flew them low over the lava lake or the summit of the volcano. Unlike my sire, I didn't throw any of them in—I merely frightened them, then dropped them a day or two's travel from their villages, so they might return with the terrible tale of the *His Evilness*, the Demon King.

Come to think of it, lately there has been an influx of new missives for me to ignore—far more than usual. A new round of terror might be in order.

My Omega's soft voice interrupts my thoughts. "What are you thinking about? You're so quiet."

"When I was of age, my father took me on long flights to show me every part of Pyreda, since it would one day be my kingdom. Once, he left me at the border without food or water, to see if I could find my way home."

Renee's gasp is audible.

"It took me three days. I got a cramp in my wing, and crashed to the ground. Unable to fly, I had no choice but to walk. My mother was livid. But a few moon-cycles later, my father did it again."

"Why?"

"To see if I'd learned my lesson. And it worked. I learned to draw upon the deep power of the land and use magic to create a portal. I returned before the suns had even reached their midday height."

"That's an awful thing to do to a child." Her fingertips are stroking my chest as if to soothe me.

"He was a demon. We don't coddle our young."

"But you wouldn't be so harsh with your own child. Would you?"

I give a noncommittal half-shrug. Since I have no intentions of becoming a father, the question is moot.

The snow clouds are drifting closer. My little Omega's face is pinched, either with thought or from the cold. There's a tug in my chest—must be from the exertion. I'm not as young as I used to be.

"It's time for us to return." I dip lower, finding a warm draft of air, and ride the current back to the castle.

To my relief, Renee relaxes in my arms. She wasn't upset, simply cold.

But as soon as I set her down, she steps away, putting some distance between us. I want to reach for her, but pride stays my hand. There's a twinge beneath my breastbone, a discordant note jarring the melody of the bond.

My Omega is not happy. Why? Haven't I done all that she requested? An uncomfortable silence accompanies us to the great hall. I'm the first to break it. "Renee."

"I need a hot shower," she murmurs, and slips through the door.

"Come to me when you are done," I command. A *jynx* appears in the doorway, waiting to be summoned. I wave it closer.

It drops a scroll into my hand. On a whim, desperate to distract myself, instead of tossing it on the pile, I unroll it and scan the careful script. It's a plea from one of the village elders, asking for ways in which they can appease both me and the volcano, to ensure it stays quiet forever. They also ask for a blessing on their crops. Barely anyone can remember the last decent harvest. It is said the seasons around my birth were considered bountiful, but the crops have declined ever since. *Please, Your Evilness.*

With a frustrated sigh, I toss the scroll into the fireplace and snap my fingers. Flames shoot up, incinerating the missive.

How can I ensure the volcano remains quiet, when my own moods are in turmoil? It's Renee's fault. I never felt so unsettled before she came along. One moment she's joyful, the next, she withdraws, stepping away from me when I would reach for her.

My frustration grows as I pace up and down the hall. I give her everything she asks for—even if she does sometimes have to wait a while. Why is she still not satisfied? What more could I do? Is this some kind of a test? Does she retreat on purpose to make me chase her?

I halt mid-step, absently stroking my braided beard. Renee adores being dominated—the crueler I am, the wetter she gets. Perhaps this is her way of telling me she wants me to be more her Master, less kind and gentle. She's never sullen or sad when my cock's inside her.

I lick my canines and raise my chin. *Females are tricky*, my father once said. *They say one thing, and mean another.* But while their words can lie, their bodies always tell the truth.

Renee is always asking questions, making requests… and even though I give her answers, and grant those wishes, she disobeyed my simple rule not to let go of me mid-flight. Now, instead of spending the rest of the day showing me her gratitude—as she promised—she has disappeared. Nobody needs this long to take a shower.

Taking a deep breath to combat my growing temper, I exhale slowly before setting out to find her. It's time to remind her I'm in charge.

She's in her bedroom, wrapped in a bathing cloth. She should be getting ready for me but she stands unmoving, frowning at the floor. In the bond between us, there's a quiet ache.

"Pet?"

She doesn't hear me right away, so I call her name. When that doesn't shake her from her reverie, I resort to the one thing that never fails: growling. Arousal floods the bond, washing everything else away.

She gasps, her eyes darkening, rising to meet mine. "Master?"

I hold out my hand. "You promised to show me your gratitude."

THIRTEEN

Renee

Today was wonderful. I thought that taking a flight together would be a good way to learn more about Krav, and it was. I had hoped to hear his stance on having kids, but after that story he told me about his father, it didn't seem like the right moment. Does he realize how abusive his dad was?

Krav seems to assume cruel behavior is normal for demons, but he wouldn't treat a child like that, would he? While we haven't discussed how he'd parent his own offspring, I've seen him with Plutus. He'd be a good dad.

Sure, he has a lot of rough edges, but he's trying. If he dropped the whole *Master of The Universe but Especially You* act—at least outside the bedroom—he'd be the guy of my dreams. I've felt closer to him since he claimed me.

And apparently the bond created by his bite does a lot more than just scar my shoulder and tie us together. He said I should now be able to *feel the land through him*, whatever that means. Share in his magical, kingly powers.

The downside to all this alien sorcery is that I can't tell whether my feelings are mine, or his, or just Ulfarri biology.

If a soul-bond is like their version of marriage, does that mean I'm his queen now? Does that even matter if he continues to treat me like a pet?

I have so many questions. Krav often seems irritated when I ask them. A part of me wants to keep the peace and stay quiet. But shutting up about my feelings and tolerating all kinds of behavior from my man sure as hell didn't work for me back on Earth. If there's one silver lining in my current situation, it has to be this: Pyreda is my chance at a fresh start.

Strange that it took a trip to a different freaking *planet* to get me the best sex of my life, but I'm rolling with it. If being here also clinches me the man—or demon—of my dreams and family I've always wanted, well, that would just be the icing, cherry, *and* sprinkles on the sundae.

A dark rumble draws me out of my reverie. Krav looms in the doorway, framed by his arched, imposing wings. His tail lashes the air behind him, as it always does when he's getting ready to pounce on me. He can stand still and menacing, but his tail betrays his mood.

His growl vibrates through every fiber of my body, and a bolt of desire makes my pussy clench. Wetness trickles down the insides of my thighs. The air fills with the heady scent of our combined arousal.

"You promised to show me your gratitude." He extends a hand tipped with wicked claws. I have to be careful when I take it, or I'll slice myself on their razor-sharp edges. But I'll still take it, even when his touch promises both pleasure and pain. Especially then.

I lift my chin, feeling small and vulnerable, naked except for one of the bizarre cloths they use for towels around here. He's so massive compared to me, his horns and wings making him twice as tall as I am. A creature born of nightmares. If he'd appeared in my bedroom back home, I'd have hollered blue murder and busted a hole in the wall to make my escape.

Here, in my new reality, I want to climb him like a tree—a big, demonic tree from hell.

I drop the towel. The fire flares in his mystic topaz eyes. I pose for a moment, letting him drink me in. My skin is flushed from the bath. My hair is still wet, and now, thanks to his incessant growling, my pussy is dripping onto the rug.

His hand is still extended. Unfurling one finger, he beckons. "Come to me, pet."

My heart pounding, I drop to all fours and crawl to him. It should be humiliating, crawling naked across a room, but my clit is throbbing. Once I'm at his feet, I hesitate a moment before rising to tall knees and reaching for his belt.

"Good girl," Krav murmurs. "Show me what a good little cocksucker you are."

His words go straight to my groin, stoking the fire between my legs. It seems to take forever to undo his belt and peel his breeches far enough down his muscular thighs to free his dick. While I've done this before, it's still intimidating. His shaft jerks, huge and purple and lined with those hard ridges. If Satan designed a dildo, it would look like this.

I lick my lips and gaze up at him pleadingly, but he doesn't move to help me. His black beard hides his cruel smile.

When I reach for his cock, he tugs me back by my hair. "Lips and tongue only."

His delicious musk makes my senses swim. Angling my head, I lick up one side of his shaft and down the other. I can't see his face, but I can picture him staring down at me, pretending to be impervious to the pleasure he's feeling. The pleasure I'm giving him. His feedback comes in the form of tiny shifts in his posture, the creak of his wings, and his fingers clenching in my hair. At least he's retracted those claws.

I delve my tongue into the notch in the tip of his cock, savoring the sweet and salty flavor. He tastes so good. I stretch my mouth over the crown, and hum. A jolt runs through him and his wings flap with a heavy leather sound. Guiding my head, he takes control, forcing himself deeper into my throat. I relax and let his magic take over. He has to be using it—there's no way I could take him this deep otherwise. I moan, and the sound hums along his length. His fingers tighten painfully in my hair, and his cock pulses and starts to expand further, the base stretching my lips. His knot. Jerking his hips back until he's halfway out, he comes with a roar, his rhythmic spurts flooding my mouth, sliding down my throat. The flavor rockets through me, driving me wild. I snake my tongue around the head of his cock again, lapping up every drop. It's too good to waste.

"Enough," he mutters, tugging me off him by my hair. "Crawl to the bed, pet."

I pout and he strokes the side of my face, scooping up a stray drop of cum and feeding it to me.

"You broke one of my rules while we were flying. It's time for your punishment." Using my hair as a leash, Krav leads me to the bed, his tail flicking my bare ass as I crawl. Once there, he tugs me up to fold my upper body over the high mattress. I press my burning cheek to the cool sheets, breathless, both dreading and excited about what might come next.

My demon lover wastes no time. The end of his tail probes my throbbing pussy and I arch my back, willing him to go deeper. Instead, infuriatingly, he slips it back out and travels higher, caressing my crack for a tantalizing second before driving deep into my ass. I let out a groan at the forbidden yet delicious sensation. Once more reaching for my hair, Krav tilts my head back to stare up at him.

"Since you enjoy being spanked so much, I've decided a little humiliation might be more effective at teaching you a lesson. That's why your punishment is this: you will come with my tail deep in your ass. Now rub yourself against the bed."

How and why is this so freaking hot? My face on fire, I rise to my tiptoes so my pussy's pressed against the mattress. Krav guides my movements, his tail pistoning in and out of me until I'm rocking forward with each thrust, grinding my clit against the bunched blankets.

"So beautiful. I wish you could see yourself like that." His tone is gentle. "My naked, desperate pet, forced to soak the bed with your slick since you haven't earned my cock yet." Despite—or maybe because of—my shame, my arousal spirals higher at his mocking words. It feels wrong to reach for a climax with a giant alien appendage deep in my ass, and yet I'm already so close. I hold myself still, quivering.

"Faster, pet." Krav rakes his claws gently down my spine, and I shiver. "Give me a show." He claps my ass-cheeks around his invading tail. Each spank sends a spear of pleasure through my core. "That's it," he snarls, increasing his pace.

"Please," I whimper, not sure what I'm asking for. This feels so depraved—and yet so good.

"You can do it, sweet one," Krav croons. "Come for me. I want to feel this tight little asshole pulsate around my tail."

That does it. My climax comes from deep in my core with such intensity, I collapse, every muscle in my sex contracting violently.

I want to lie there forever, panting, hiding my face in the crook of my arm, letting the white-hot pleasure ebb away slowly… but Krav has other ideas.

Gripping me by my hair at the nape of my neck, he tugs me back up to all fours. His tail slides out of me, then the tip of something much thicker and—lord help me—covered with ridges presses lightly against that same area. His cock.

"You're so beautiful when you lose control like that," he says. "See how good it feels when you obey? And now it's my turn. You're mine, pet. Every part of you belongs to me, which is why I'm going to come deep in your ass."

"Oh fuck," I groan. "Master, I don't think—"

"You're not here to think," he interrupts me. "You're here to feel. To trust that I won't harm you."

"But it's too—"

He caresses my buttock as if trying to reassure me. "Magic, remember?" he whispers. "I promise it will be slick enough, and that you'll enjoy it. All I want you to do is trust… be a good girl, and take it…"

He always knows just what to say to make me melt, damn him. "Then please, just keep talking to me," I whisper.

"You took my tail in your ass so well." His low, gravelly voice makes me shiver. "You can do the same with my cock, sweetheart. I know your slick cunt is aching to have me inside it, but I've already pumped that hole full of my cum so many times. I've sprayed down your throat—and you swallowed it so obediently. Now there's one place left to fill…"

I'm panting, twisting the sheets between my fingers as he begins to push, invading me, impaling me, forcing his way inside.

"Ulf, that's so tight," he groans, gripping my hips to hold me in place. He retracted his talons so his fingertips dig into my flesh. "Relax. Concentrate on how good it feels." One of his hands slides down between my legs. "You're so slick…"

He swirls two fingertips around the entrance to my pussy before laying them over my clit and rubbing gently. I gasp.

"That's it," he croons, "concentrate on how big and swollen this little bud is getting. I can feel it throbbing." He's going deeper into my ass, splitting me in two. "But you need to relax. You're not allowed to come yet. No clenching. You hear me?"

I whimper. Being told I'm not allowed to orgasm always sends me to the very edge.

"I'm halfway in," he continues. "When I'm all the way in, you can come. But not before then. Just relax into it and focus on my fingers…"

He's dragging my clit back and forth in the most delicious way. My pussy flutters.

"Nu-uh," he snarls, startling me. "Don't you dare disobey me."

"Fuck, Master, please…"

He slides deeper with a grunt, the sharp ache in my rear hole only magnifying how wonderful his fingertips feel between my thighs. "Almost there, sweet thing. Just a little further to go."

I whimper as he continues his inexorable invasion, focusing all my attention on keeping my muscles relaxed as the pleasure spirals higher… higher…

"I wish you could see this, pet. Your ass frames my cock so perfectly as I stretch it wide. No, don't move. Be still and let it happen. You can take it… Ulf… take all of me…"

Krav lets out a primal roar which hurls me over the edge. I howl as the orgasm overtakes me, pulsing waves of pleasure snatching the breath from my lungs.

I'm still coming as he gives one final, hard thrust, the burning ache amplifying the throbbing in my clit. His cock jerks inside me, almost lifting me off the bed with the force of his climax as he fills my ass with rhythmic spurts.

We collapse together—me on my belly, my Master on top of me, his skin searing mine. He's panting, his warm breath fluttering across my hair. His dick is still buried in my ass, cum leaking out around it, dribbling down to pool below my groin.

"I couldn't hold out any longer," Krav murmurs, nuzzling my neck. "I didn't even go all the way in."

"Are you sure? Only I felt like the tip was about to hit my tonsils." I giggle, then wince as Krav chuckles, shifting inside me.

"I'm sure. I didn't want to knot your ass—"

"Thank god."

"Not the first time, at least." Another chuckle. "You did so well, sweetheart, even though you came too soon."

"I could hardly wait until you were all the way in if you weren't planning to go that far!" I grumble.

"True, but you didn't know that."

The amusement in his voice reassures me. "I couldn't help it," I confess. "You know how the noises you make affect me."

"I know—and I adore it." He nuzzles my neck. "You took me in your ass so well. I'm proud of you."

Contentment licks up my chest, and I smile into the sheets. "Thank you."

"But we're not done."

I try to work out if there's any part of my body that isn't aching. The orgasms are worth it, but they sure are draining. Seems like women need a refractory period too, when the sex is good enough. "We're not?"

"Oh, no."

"I don't think I can move right now," I mumble as he withdraws from me, then I wince at the sharp ache as his cock pops out of my tight hole.

He takes pity on me and scoops me up, carrying me like a bride to the bathing chamber. "A hot bath, I think, and then some food."

Relief makes me sag in his hold. "That sounds perfect."

He kisses the top of my head. "You're perfect."

My heart sings at the compliment. Even though I'm exhausted and starving, I'm filled with happiness. "You're not too shabby yourself," I tell him.

Krav doesn't reply but when I glance up at his face, his lips are curved up, that gorgeous dimple of his revealed by a beaming smile.

<hr>

DUSK HAS FALLEN by the time we're done soaking our tired, sore muscles. We end up having dinner in bed, curled up together. He feeds me pieces of *kiktu*—one of my favorite Ulfarri fruits—a dark gleam in his eyes as I lick the juices off his fingers. His cock hardens and inwardly, I groan. While I adore how much he desires me, I'm exhausted. I need to distract him.

I reach up to touch his horns and he stills. "They're sensitive, aren't they?" He nods, and I run a gentle finger down the ridged surface. He shudders, and a purr bursts from his chest. It's brief, but still enough to fill me with a deep sense of relaxation. I've learned his growl arouses me, his purr soothes me, and his chest feels like home. Rolling onto my side, I press my cheek to hear his heartbeat, slow and steady.

His tail strokes my butt.

"What about your wings? Are they sensitive too?"

He unfurls one and stretches it over me. The light from the glow orbs illuminates the map of veins and sinew in the leathery expanse. I raise my hand then hesitate. "Can I?"

He nods and I brush my fingertips over the glossy surface. It's warm to the touch.

"You feel that?"

"Yes." His wing quivers under my caress, and I revel in the discovery. He looks so intimidating but now I know the truth: he feels everything. Maybe that's why he fights so hard to keep everyone at wing's length?

Krav lets me explore as much as I want until I yawn so

widely, my jaw cracks. He commands the *jynx* to remove the empty plates and dim the orbs.

I stretch out on the bed. He tucks the sheets around me, and I drink in his scent—smoke and chocolate, like a burned s'more. I try to fill my lungs with him before he leaves.

After he bit me to create the soul-bond, he slept beside me until the next morning and I was elated, hoping it was a sign of change. That his walls were coming down. Unfortunately, it seems I was wrong. The following night, he went back to his own bed as soon as he thought I was asleep… and now he's getting ready to leave me again.

Tired of sleeping alone, longing to be held some more, I summon all my courage and reach for him. "Please… will you stay with me? All night?"

He hesitates, and with a sinking heart, I wait for him to shake his head and stride away. Instead, he leans towards me and lets me pull him down beside me again.

I wriggle with excitement, unable to contain my smile.

"Pet," he rasps. My butt is grinding against his cock. "I want to take you again, but you need your rest. *We* need our rest."

He's right. Fatigue has settled heavy in my limbs. The sex marathon wore me out.

I can't believe I'm spooning with a demon. We're both on our sides, facing the wall of windows. Mount Vracor is a dark silhouette against the starry night.

"The volcano isn't as active as it was when I first arrived here."

"Hrmph." Krav sounds annoyed, as if the lazy mountain offends him. "For now, it merely slumbers." He trails his claws over me before retracting them so he can hold me tight. "Shall I tell you the story of Mount Vracor?"

"There's a story?"

His voice is low and rough, falling into a lilt like a lullaby. "Long ago, Ulf made the world. He formed the nine kingdoms and the wastelands, and fashioned the hills, plains, oceans, and all the creatures upon it, including the Alphas, the Betas, and the Omegas. And when he was done, he made to move on, but the land at the heart of his creation was on fire. It was the place where he had made all the life, and it burned with the vestiges of his power. Each kingdom needed a king, but who could rule a land of fire?"

Krav caresses my side, his fingertips playing over my ribs. It would distract me if his voice were not so mesmerizing. The heat radiating off his huge body envelops me in a cocoon of contentment.

"So Ulf raised up a mountain called Vracor—which means heart of the demon—and forged his creation fires once more. He spoke his intent, reached into the burning lava, and drew out his final creation from the very heart of the volcano. The creature was an Alpha, tall and well-formed, with skin the color of cooling lava and the purple sands of the desert. It had horns, fangs and claws, and wings and a tail." Krav's tail coils possessively around my ankle. "It was a demon, the first king of Pyreda. My ancestor."

He pauses long enough, I feel like I'm supposed to say something. "Whoa."

He chuckles, and I snuggle closer. "And that is how demons came to be. Ulf left Mount Vracor as a symbol of his power—and ours. It is said the volcano is attuned to the king's moods."

"Really?"

My body shifts as he shrugs. "That's what my father told me. It would erupt whenever he flew into one of his rages."

I wince. More evidence Krav's dad was the worst. "That's awful."

"He was a demon. What do you expect?"

"That's no excuse for being an asshole."

"The fires burn hotter inside of us. We are forged in flames." His hand glides down my hip, his fingertips brushing tantalizingly close to my sex. And I'm wet for him all over again.

I look over my shoulder to peek at Krav, but he has his eyes closed.

"Sleep, pet," he orders, as if he knows I'm watching him. "It's been a long day, and we need our rest."

He's not wrong. I close my eyes obediently, trying to quiet my thoughts. I keep going back to what Emma said, about Alphas being all about the breeding, and how desperate Khan was to get her pregnant. Krav is an Alpha, too, and yet I still don't even know if he wants a family. Whenever the subject comes up, he skirts around it.

While it's still early days for us as a couple, ever since I found out humans and Ulfarri can breed successfully, I've repeatedly caught myself fantasizing about it—staying here with Krav and starting a family of my own. Giving him a chance to prove that bad parenting cycles can be broken—even if you are a demon.

Krav acts all big and bad but when he's in a gentle mood, he's the warmest, most affectionate, caring guy. Having spent so much time with him, I no longer believe he's incapable of empathy. Why else would he warm my hands or bring me food without being asked? I've done enough therapy to understand how behavior patterns are formed, and he had the worst role model in his father. Add to that the fact he's never had a proper relationship before, and it's no wonder he blows hot and cold. He's probably confused as all get out.

I snuggle back against his comforting warmth. He agreed to spend the night with me. He took me out for an adventure. He's certainly trying. I just need to be patient.

On the other hand, honey, you ain't getting any younger. Try as I might to push that thought away, it keeps bubbling back up. While it might be prudent to wait some more, I need to find out whether Krav would be willing to have a kid with me.

I've spent the last year or two struggling to accept the likelihood of being childless forever so now, if there's a chance I can have the family I've always wanted with a guy I'm crazy about, I owe it to myself to try. I read somewhere that a woman's fertility starts dropping in her thirties so it might take a little longer—especially if he keeps coming in the wrong dang places, sheesh—but then again, I still menstruate, everyone keeps saying how fertile Omegas are, and my body feels different in so many ways since I got shot up with that serum. Maybe our rutting is enough, but maybe we could use a little extra help. Emma kindly offered to put me in touch with someone—a *magician,* I still grin at the term—who will hopefully have answers to all my questions about this. It would be foolish not to take advantage of the opportunity when there's nothing to lose and everything to gain.

Krav and I just need to be on the same page about this.

I close my eyes, feeling somewhat calmer now I've made the decision: I'll talk to him about it in the morning.

The blanket has slipped below my waist but it doesn't matter. I'm being snuggled by my living, breathing hot water bottle. His light, rhythmic snores soothe me like a lullaby, and I plummet into sleep.

FOURTEEN

Krav

I AWAKEN to the sound of weeping. I'm on my feet—wings half unfurled, claws extended—before I realize it was a dream. My pet lies twisted in the sheets, her face scrunched in sleep. There's a faint tinge of anxiety in the bond between us, a discordant note in the normally harmonious hum.

I long to stay beside her, which is why I make myself go. But the pain in my chest doesn't ease.

It grows worse.

By midday, I've escaped to my study to see whether making some music will help the ache in the bond threatening to suffocate me.

It was a mistake to sleep beside my pet. Everything I've done to remain in control was swept away when I gave in to her request and spent the night by her side. If I'm not careful, she'll get ideas—think she has power over me.

I will not be ruled by an Omega. I will not succumb to weakness and tell myself it's *love*, as others do.

Khan is a prime example. He's a successful Alpha king, one who commanded entire fleets of spaceships, whose reputation preceded him throughout the galaxy, and whose name struck terror into the hearts of foes, and yet the other day, he merely sat meekly beside Emma, reduced to a silent observer. A trinket on her arm. A shadow of what an Alpha should be.

Pathetic. I hear the insult in my father's voice. He hovers incessantly in the back of my mind, sneering at anything he judges to be weak. He would make some allowances for my behavior in rut, but my longing to draw Renee close, to keep her with me always?

No sex is worth the headache of an uppity female.

He would advise me to put space between myself and the Omega. To spend time away from her until I can cease my thoughts' constant orbit around her. She has become the suns and moons of my life, a disturbance bigger than an erupting volcano.

I try everything to make her happy—taking her on a flight, showering her with gifts, and learning everything that gives her pleasure purely to give her more of it—and yet she is never truly content. There are recurring spells of disquiet in the bond. I felt a faint one last night, and this morning, when I left her to sleep longer. When she woke to find me gone, her disappointment was like a knife slicing through my breastbone. The pain flared to a sharp peak, then faded to a dull ache. It's still there, an acid corroding the connection between us.

Claiming her wasn't a mistake—I needed to mark her as mine, bind her to me always. What I didn't anticipate was the depth of emotions the bond would make me suffer through. There must be a way to dull them, if not remove them completely.

Perhaps I shouldn't spend so much time with her outside of the bedroom. After all, I don't spend every waking moment with Plutus. Maybe that's why he's always so happy to see me.

I pluck a discordant note on the strings of my *hriox*, filling the room with a jarring twang.

My father always insisted that females should know their place. Renee does not, and it is my fault. By dining with her, having endless discussions with her, allowing her to meet another Hoo-man, I've obviously confused her. She is my *pet*. My plaything. A morsel for my sexual appetite. Nothing more. I must remind her of her place not with the physical dominance she so adores, but by withdrawing more. Spending more time as I used to—in my own company, relishing the solitude.

From now on, no matter how prettily she pleads, we will sleep apart. She will wait for me in her bedchamber, her thoughts focused on how she can entice me to stay by her side. And with space and time away from her, I will regain control over myself. No more a servant of the soul-bond, but a master.

In my mind's eye, my father nods. He approves of this plan.

The *hriox* sings under my fingers, and I fall into playing a familiar melody. Beautiful, and sad. I play and play, ignoring the twinge in my chest that makes it hard to breathe.

"Here you are." Renee stands in the doorway, her face half in shadow.

My fingers slip on the strings and the air echoes with the last sour note.

"I was looking for you." She takes a small step forward then hesitates, her expression unreadable.

"And here I am," I say, setting the *hriox* aside.

"What's that?" Her gaze flicks to the ornate silver instrument.

"A *hriox*. My mother's. She often played it." The melancholy tune I just played was one of her favorites.

My pet approaches me slowly. "Maybe you could play it for me?"

"Another time."

She rubs her head. "Krav... can we talk? There's something I've been thinking about."

I make no move to encourage her. I ache to reach for her, hold her close, but I will myself to be still. To treat her coldly. As a demon should. As my father would desire.

"It was after that orb call we had with Khan and Emma." She settles on a nearby stool. "It's about the whole kids thing." Her gaze is on her hands, clenched in her lap. "See, I never thought it would be possible for me. First, because of my age, and because I couldn't find any guy worthy of being my baby daddy back home. And then here, I ruled it out because I figured... well, we're not even the same species. Sure, we can fuck, but I never thought we could..."

"Breed successfully?" I suggest when she trails off. My tone is deliberately cool. Disinterested. Conversations like this make me uncomfortable.

"Well, yeah." She bites her lip. "But now I know otherwise. And it's got me thinking... do you... would you ever... I mean, would you be happy if I got pregnant?" Her eyes are intent on me now. The ache in the bond is intensifying. I want to rub my chest but force myself to remain still.

"I have no desire for children," I tell her. "So it won't ever happen."

She blinks. "Won't ever happen? How can you know for sure?"

"Because I prevent it."

"I'm sorry, what?"

"The same way I use a little magic to heal you after, to ensure I can fit inside you without causing you harm, I use magic to prevent any... consequences. To prevent my seed from taking root."

Her eyes are wide, her fingers creep to her lips. They're trembling. "Why?"

"As I said, I don't want progeny. Demons don't make good parents. Ulf knows, my father proved that."

"But… why didn't you tell me you were doing that?"

I'm baffled by her question. It never occurred to me. "Why should I?" She seems to be waiting for more of an explanation so I cast about. "You're my pet, not my queen."

She flinches as if I'd struck her. Her eyes are glistening. "All this time, I thought you were just emotionally unavailable. But now, I'm starting to wonder… do you even care about me?"

A crack forms in my chest at the accusation, but I infuse my voice with frost. "Of course I care. I see that you are sheltered and fed. I conjure pretty things for you. Ensure you're clothed—albeit to my liking." My gaze darts to her bare legs. "What else could you possibly desire?"

"That's just it." She rises and paces past me, knotting her fingers together. "I thought I could be content with that. Living here, surrounded by magic, with a guy who can fly—and who lets me explore my kinkiest fantasies with him. But I want more." She stops in front of the window. Her posture changes—her shoulders draw back, her chin lifts. "I deserve more."

See? my father's ghost whispers. *She forgets her place. You must constantly remind her by remaining stoic and setting boundaries because if you give her any leeway, she will take over your life.*

In the back of my mind, I hear doors slamming. My father stomping through the halls. Someone is weeping.

I blink, force myself back to the present.

Renee is gazing out of the window, unaware of my reverie. "All my life, I've settled. Made do. But heck, I'm on an alien planet, living with a demon. And it turns out I could have everything I want with him. A child, maybe two. A family. Why shouldn't I go for it?"

"Because it's my decision, not yours. I am the master. You are my pet."

"Is that all I am to you?"

I clench my fists by my sides, steeling myself. "Yes." The statement is an agonizing blade which knifes through my organs, slicing them in two. But I let no sign of it show on my face. If Renee turns to look at me now, she will see nothing but a cold, hard Alpha. A king. A demon.

In my memory, the sound of weeping fades, replaced by a distant rumble. The thunderous sound grows louder. I feel it in my bones, cracking and surging. But it's not coming from within. I'm sensing the upheaval in the land.

Boom! The room shakes. The *hriox* judders off the table, smashing to the ground.

Without hesitating, I leap to Renee, wrapping her up tight in my wings. She holds on to me, burying her face in my chest. Shelves fall, chairs and stools tip over, the ceiling cracks. Dust rains down.

We cling to each other for long moments after the aftershocks die away. I want to keep her pressed up against me, but settle for steadying her. *I'm not coddling her. Omegas are fragile. I want to keep her safe.*

Renee is the first to speak. "Was that…"

"The volcano." I crane my head to see out of the window. Thick, dark smoke billows from Mount Vracor once more.

"That's not a good sign, is it?" She pushes away from me. I'm reluctant to let her go, but my newly made resolution forces me to remain still as she hurries to the window, careful to avoid the debris. "Is it going to blow?"

I shrug. "It could… any day now."

She whirls on me, the color rising in her speckled cheeks. "Don't you even care?"

"Why should I?"

"If the volcano erupts, people will die! Their village is right in the path of that thing—"

"They should have thought of that before they settled underneath an Ulfdamn volcano."

"Where were they supposed to settle? Next to the lake of lava? It's not like there's anywhere around here that's completely safe. This whole place is a hellscape."

Her accusations grate on me. "Welcome to my kingdom."

"Exactly. *Your* kingdom. You're the king. You have a responsibility—"

"The Pyredii must be strong enough to fend for themselves! I will not tolerate weakness!" I roar.

All the color ebbs from Renee's face. "And there it is. You don't care at all. Not about them." Her voice breaks. "Not about me." She fingers the fire-stone set in the collar around her neck.

I take a breath, ready to say something cutting but her eyes are brimming. The words shrivel on my lips as a fat tear escapes and trickles down her pale, freckled cheek.

"Damnit," she says, wiping it away with a sniff. "Never let 'em see you cry."

I've never seen her weep before. There's a searing ache in my chest. "Pet—"

Ignoring me, she stands in the wreckage of the room, sobbing so hard her shoulders shake, her face in her hands. Her sorrow lances through the bond, screeching like nails raked down a smooth rock surface.

On instinct, I begin to purr.

"No!" she barks, raising red-rimmed eyes to meet mine. "Don't. I don't want your fucking pity!"

Is that what I feel? I stop purring. "It's not pity. It's just to soothe—"

She interrupts me again, holding up a trembling hand. "Whatever it is, I don't want it. This is what got me so messed up in the first place. You blowing hot and cold, showing hints of affection, when in reality..." She exhales shakily and wipes her cheeks with the back of her hand. "I wish I had a dang tissue, a rag, anything to blow my nose."

I make a square of the softest cloth and hand it to her.

"Thanks. Ugh." She presses it to her face. A moment later, she raises her head again. Her eyes are still wet but her sobs have stopped.

Females, my father would say, shaking his head. He would always stomp away, slamming doors in his wake, drowning out the sounds of weeping.

Squaring my shoulders, I lift my chin and point to the doorway with a single talon. "Go to your chambers, and stay there. You will not leave them until I summon you."

Renee scoffs. "You think I'll come when you call? Don't hold your breath." She picks her way through the fallen detritus and glides through the open door. Her graceful exit makes me feel worse.

Slamming doors. Stomping boots. The hriox's *sad song, accompanied by muffled sobs.* I clutch my head, willing the memories to stop. My claws tear into my scalp.

When I lower my hands, the castle is silent. Renee is long gone. And where there used to be warmth and light in the bond, there's nothing left but emptiness.

As it should be.

***

Renee

I curl up on my bed, but there are no more tears. Words can't describe how upset I am. The more I try to get closer to Krav, to get him to open up to me, the more he retreats. And that conversation just now was the final straw.

It was hard for me to approach him about the kid thing, especially to admit that I want one… with him… and then he just casually told me that not only has he been actively using birth control—without my knowledge—he didn't even understand why it would be any of my business!

What the actual fuck?

It wasn't intentional deceit, either. He didn't look like a guy caught in a lie. He genuinely didn't think he needed to tell me.

Why?

Because he doesn't think I'm important enough. Because he doesn't see me as a partner. Because he's incapable of feeling any emotion other than pride, lust, anger, and jealousy. Four of the seven deadly sins, come to think of it.

And now his kingdom is at risk of being swallowed up by lava—the parts that aren't already covered in it, that is. I once saw a documentary on Pompeii, how the entire city was devastated by the erupting volcano in just fifteen minutes. Now the poor Pyredii are facing a similar fate. I wish I could do something.

Infuriatingly, I can't even help myself. I've been sent to my room like a naughty child. So as far as I'm concerned, Krav can go fuck himself. Literally. I will not be his *good little pet* anymore.

My chest aches. The sweet music in the bond between us has faded to nothing but a hollow moan. Am I going to feel the chill of this emptiness forever? Things could have been so different. We could have been happy, if he'd just let me in. Treated me like a freaking *equal.* Instead, all I can do is burrow under the covers and throw myself a pity party.

My attention is drawn to a flashing light beside my bed. It's coming from one of the weird orbs that dim or grow bright depending on the time of day.

"Hello?" a familiar voice calls. It's high and feminine. Human. British. And it's coming from the orb.

"Emma?" I scoot closer to the sphere, and my new friend's pretty face appears. I had no idea my nightlight could double as an alien video chat device.

"Yep, it's me," she says. "Just me. Hope I'm not disturbing you, but I was worried about you after our call the other day."

"You're not disturbing me at all. In fact, your timing couldn't be better!" The empathy in her voice is about to set me off weeping all over again. Hopefully she won't notice how sore my eyes are.

She leans forward, peering at me. "You okay? You look like you've been crying."

It's so typical. I hardly *ever* cry. Today was the first time since I arrived, I think. Phillip once accused me of using tears as emotional manipulation, and that was when I swore never to cry because of—or in front of—a man again. But damnit, it took me ages to make peace with the thought that I'll never be a mom. So to have that carrot dangled in front of me again out of nowhere, with a guy I'm crazy about, no less, only for it to be then yanked away by the same guy… it was too much. Krav just looked stunned when I started sobbing. Figures. "I'm fine," I tell Emma. "Didn't sleep too well. Eyes are a bit dry."

It's obvious from her expression that she doesn't believe me but she doesn't press the issue.

"How are you doing?" I ask. "Everything okay in, uh, your kingdom?"

"Altrim." She grins. "Yes. We're fine. I just wanted to see how you were doing."

"Aww, that's sweet." I extend a finger to touch the glowing sphere in front of me, then hesitate. It's emanating heat. Is it some sort of transparent metal? Glass? "I still can't believe we can talk through these… orb thingies."

"I know, right?"

"Although I shouldn't be surprised, what with all the magic that exists here."

Emma's eyes light up. "Isn't it amazing? Do your paintings move, too?"

"Huh?" I'm confused.

"I love to paint, always have," she explains. "Soon after we met, Khan got a local artist to teach me how to use their magic paint. Now my pictures literally move!"

"In what way?"

"Leaves rustle on trees, lakes ripple, that kind of thing. It completely rejuvenated my passion for art." She tucks a stray lock of blonde hair behind her ear. "Sorry. I'm rambling. So what kind of magic do you have there?"

"I don't know the scope of it yet but Krav uses it to make me things. He can conjure stuff out of thin air. Pillows. Clothes. Inanimate stuff." *My collar.* I swallow against the lump in my throat.

"That's so cool! Rose and her mate have some magic powers, too, I believe—I watched them float high into the air on this big glass platform once. Have you been able to conjure anything yourself?"

"Me? No."

"Apparently, it's one of the signs of a soul-bond. The kings around here get powers from their respective lands. Some sort of symbiosis. And then their mates—queens—get powers too, via the claiming bond. You did tell us Krav claimed you, right?"

I'm not following this conversation very well. "Um, I think so. I mean, he bit me, said we were bound together now, but…" The sorrow chokes me, like I've got glass stuck in my throat. "Let's just say it's not going well."

"I'm sorry." Emma's expression reflects the pain I feel. "I guess congratulations are not in order?"

"No. They are not." I rub my chest. "For one thing, he refuses to treat me like an equal. I'm all about being submissive in bed, but outside of that, I want a partner… ideally to have kids with him. It's so typical. I finally meet the guy I could see myself starting a family with, and then it turns out he doesn't want that. In fact, he's been actively preventing it. Without my knowledge."

Emma's blue gaze is full of compassion. "Oh, babe. I'm sorry."

"It's okay," I whisper. I press my eyes as if I can push my tears back in. "I'm dealing with it."

There's a long pause. "Would you leave him, if you could?" Her voice is so soft, I wonder if I heard right.

"I wouldn't know how." It's easier to focus on the logistics than the emotional implications.

"We could find a way. I'll think of something. You'd just have to trust me."

"He'd never let me go." The scar on my neck throbs. "He's a possessive bastard."

"He's an Alpha. They all are." Emma sighs, tapping her chin. "Still, I'm certain we could get you out—and even keep him away, if it came down to it. Pyreda doesn't have a standing army. There's no reason for it—no one wants to claim an inhospitable land full of fire."

My first instinct is to defend this kingdom, but I swallow my response. Why should I care what she says about this place? After all, it's true. "I really appreciate your offer to help but I wouldn't want you to put yourself out. Or put yourself in any kind of danger."

She scoffs. "We wouldn't be in any danger. Unlike Krav, we *do* have an army. And Khan is a warrior like no other." I've noticed she glows whenever she says his name.

"You're crazy about him, aren't you? Khan?"

Her eyes soften. "Yeah. I didn't like him all that much at first, but when it came down to it... I couldn't bear to leave him. The point is, he gave me the choice."

"He did?"

"Yes. And you deserve someone like that. Someone you stay with because you *want* to, not because you have to."

"You're right. I do deserve exactly that." The old Renee, Earth Renee, might not have agreed with her so readily, but I'm not that woman anymore. Give me all—or nothing. No more half-assed crap. No more being a glorified booty call. "Thanks."

"You're welcome. We humans have to stick together. Now, here's what I was thinking about your escape…"

As Emma explains her ideas, I'm torn between my head and my heart. Could I really do it? Leave the guy I've fallen for? Memories of our time together—both happy and sad—swirl though my mind like an emotional merry-go-round.

But at the end of the day, it all boils down to one thing: he doesn't love me.

And as Emma said: I deserve someone who does.

It's as simple—and heartbreaking—as that.

FIFTEEN

Krav

I PACE the halls of my castle, my anger my only companion. The sound of my stomping boots is a hollow replacement for the music in the bond. There is nothing between me and my Omega but a haze of anguish. The pain increased with every tear that spilled from her eyes, and I did nothing. She wept and I did not comfort her. She even rejected my purr.

Ever since, she's been miserable in her rooms. If I reach out, braving the torment in the bond, I can sense her weary sorrow. My talons cut into my palms. I wish I could rip into my chest and tear my heart to shreds. End this agony.

My pacing has brought me to my mother's set of rooms in her tower. I wait for my memory to play tricks on me, to hear the haunting music as she plays the *hriox*, making it weep. But for once, all is silent. I don't need the pain of old ghosts. I have my Omega's—and my own.

After our argument, I climbed to the tallest tower and prepared to hurl myself into the wind. I'd spend the day flying, terrorizing the villagers. Teach them not to look to a demon for help or comfort.

But I cannot bring myself to fly from the castle and leave Renee behind. What if she needs me? What if she's cold?

The day is chilly and overcast, with low, grey clouds. The slopes of Mount Vracor sparkle under a coat of frost. My Omega's wardrobe is not heavy enough for these frigid temperatures.

I summon the *jynx* and conjure a set of thick fur robes—one white, one pale purple like the snow—to send to her.

I avoided her this morning, so I don't know if she ate enough of the morning repast. I order the *jynx* to prepare her favorite foods, including the *leeberry*-flavored pastries she loves so much. Only when my servants report that they have given her the gifts and food, and built up her fire, do I relax.

I settle into my chair, the tips of my claws drumming the elaborately carved armrests.

Should I send for her? I could bid her sit on my lap. She would pout at first, but after a few minutes of my playing with her body, my scent surrounding her, she'd be slick and eager, desperate to have me. When we were in heat, everything was easier.

If I had just heeded my father's advice and maintained a cool distance between us, none of this would have happened. Females are happier in subservient roles, with firm boundaries.

But as soon as I think this, I hear the sad songs my mother used to play, underscored with her weeping. If my father's way was right, why did it lead to so much sorrow?

A distant roll of thunder heralds the ground's tremors. The earthquake is minor, barely shaking the room, but when I stride to the window, thick plumes of smoke spiral from Mount Vracor's summit.

The volcano is awakening.

More tremors rumble beneath my feet. Heart thumping, I race through the castle. Renee should be secure in her rooms, but if anything falls on her or she loses her balance, she could be hurt.

When I reach her chambers, I stop short. The fur robes are piled up outside her door. Beside them rests the tray of *leeberry* tarts the *jynx* prepared. My Omega is rejecting my gifts.

Another mini-quake shakes the hallway. The turmoil I feel inside is finally making its way to the volcano. It could not happen at a worse time.

I stamp on the stone and wait for the door to slide open. Nothing happens. I slam it again and again before pounding my fists on the door. "Pet?"

"Shoot, he's here!" she exclaims. Who is she talking to? Her voice is hushed, muffled by the closed door. The blood is roaring in my ears.

She's locked in but nothing will keep me from her. Unwilling to wait for the *jynx* to come and fix whatever's broken, I tear at the hinges and wrench the bronze slab aside. It knocks the pile of gifts over and crashes to the ground. Renee shrieks.

My heart hammering, I peer inside. Everything is dark except for a giant glowing circle spun by blazing magic. A portal. Beyond it, the room is furnished unlike any in my castle. The seamless stone walls of an unfamiliar palace.

Renee stands before the whirling gateway, in the dress I designed for her the day we spoke with Khan and Emma. She turns and looks at me, her eyes wet.

"Quickly," someone hisses from inside the portal. A small *Hoo-man* with a pale face and golden hair—my skin prickles as I recognize Khan's queen—beckons to my Omega.

"What is happening here?" I shout. "No!" As Renee turns, I race to catch her, but I'm too late.

She steps through the portal a mere instant before I crash against the invisible barrier.

"What's happening?" Dazed, I reach for her, but the magic

repels me. I stagger back, my wings flaring out to keep me upright. "Pet!"

My Omega scuttles further inside before turning to face me. I hammer the portal with my fists but it's futile—they just bounce off.

Renee flinches back, her green eyes wide with fear. Is she afraid of me? The notion is like a blade in my gut.

"Don't worry," Emma says. "He can't enter. I had the magicians set it so only one being can step through."

I fumble for the portal's edges as if I could pry it open, but there's nothing to hold. The ground rumbles again, but I barely hear it over the discordant twang in our bond.

"Pet? What is the meaning of this?"

"I'm leaving you." Renee's voice is defiant but she's trembling.

A crashing cacophony of ear-bleeding sounds almost deafens me. The earthquake's aftershocks have faded but I sway as if dealt a blow. "You're not. I won't allow it!" I snarl, recovering myself. I need to attack the portal, force it to admit me so I can reach my pet and drag her back to me, where she belongs, but the magic is too powerful. I cannot counter it. My wings droop as I'm overtaken by a crushing exhaustion.

Khan's queen crosses her slender arms defensively. She's so slight but the expression on her face is fierce.

I stab a talon in her direction. "This is your doing. You stole my Omega."

"You can't steal a person," Emma snaps. "Renee makes her own choices. She's not an object you can *steal*."

"Thanks, Emma. Can you give us a minute? I promise I'll be okay." Renee waits until her friend is out of sight before turning to address me. Were it not for the infuriating, invisible barrier between us, I could reach out and touch her. "She did it for me. I asked for it."

"But… why?" Confusion and anger strain my voice.

"Because you don't care about me." She reaches for her throat, curling her fingers around the collar she wears for me, the one I made for her, even as she accuses me of neglect.

"That's a lie! I do care for you. I've given you everything!" Vibrating with indignation, I point to the hallway behind me strewn with furs and *leeberry* pastries. "Food, shelter, jewels, outings—anything you want, everything you desire—"

"Everything… except what I want most. I'm just a pet to you. A booty call. I thought I could deal with it at first. You've gotta play the hand you're dealt, ya know?" She dashes her fingers across her face, swiping her tears away. "And at the start, it was a fun, sexy fantasy. I pretended none of it was real. But as time went on, I caught feelings for you. Real feelings."

"I know, pet," I say in the tone I always use to soothe her.

"No!" she snaps. "You don't know! Or you don't care. You're incapable of it. You don't want *me*. You want a plaything… a pet. But while that was fun for a little while, it's not fun anymore. I want to be more. I *deserve* to be more, goddamnit!"

This can't be happening. In a moment, I will wake up, and my beautiful Omega won't be standing beyond my reach, her face soaked with tears, her accusations ringing in my ears. Instead, she'll be curled up beside me, her freckled skin soft against mine, her sweet scent surrounding me.

She'll be in my arms. Where she belongs.

Renee

Krav is just inches away, looming tall in his full demon glory. His wings quiver and his tail lashes the air behind him. There's a deep rumbling in the distance, like the earthquakes are back. But he doesn't seem to notice them, so I focus on him.

I knew he'd be angry when he found out I was leaving—although I had hoped to be long gone before he discovered my absence. I should have known my bedroom door would be no match for him. What I didn't expect was the look on his face when he tried to reach for me through the portal. Or his expression now, as he stands in front of me. So close, and yet so far.

"I know you tried," I say softly. I have to make him understand. "Yes, you give me all the pastries and furry cloaks a girl could want. And I'll admit that being your little pet is fun… in the bedroom. But I want—no, I *deserve*—to be more than that to you, or to any guy I end up with, for that matter. I'm not Plutus. I need more than the occasional pat on the head, and handful of critters tossed my way."

Fire flares in his rainbow topaz eyes. "You can't leave me. I gave you the bite. You're my bonded mate!"

The crack in his voice is like a shard of glass through my heart but my mind is made up. "If you treated me that way, if you truly saw me as your equal, your queen, I'd agree with you," I say slowly, rubbing my chest. "But even though I've fallen in love with you, it's become clear that you can't love me back." A huge lump is sticking in my throat, and I swallow hard, trying to clear it. "Quite honestly, I don't think you're capable of it. Of seeing me as more than just a *thing* you own, along with all your other possessions. I'm not mad —I know you didn't have the best role model. And for a little while, I thought I could stick it out and stay with you anyway. But now I know for sure that I just can't. It hurts to love someone who doesn't love you back. Being around them every day… well, that's just excruciating. I can't do it anymore. I'm sorry."

The sudden hand on my arm makes me jump. Emma's come over to stand beside me.

"I knew this would happen!" Krav explodes, regaining his voice—and his temper. He turns on Emma. "This is your fault. This is why I didn't want her to meet you. I knew you'd turn her against me and persuade her to leave!"

A growl erupts from behind us, startling the crap out of me. Khan strides forward, his eyes flashing. His markings look darker, and his canines gleam menacingly. He looks ready to leap through the portal and kill Krav. I squeak, ready to scuttle out of his way, but Emma holds up a hand to halt him and gestures for me to respond.

"Neither of them is to blame," I correct Krav. "No one is. Who knows, maybe if I hadn't fallen for you, I would have been content to stay with you forever, getting my brains fucked out and amassing an enormous collection of transparent gowns. But now I'm invested, so that just wouldn't cut it anymore."

Krav's expression is like mine when I'm wrestling with my tax return. It's almost enough to make me smile. Almost. "I gave you more than that," he protests. "We spent almost every waking moment together. We talked endlessly—"

I shake my head. "*I* talked. You pretended to listen. You think I didn't see those flashes of irritation every time I asked a question? You think I didn't notice that you've never asked me anything about myself, about my past, about my hopes, fears, and dreams? That's because you're just not interested in me as a person. And that's okay. I mean, it's not okay, but… it is what it is." Blinking back the tears that are making my vision blurry, I turn to Emma. "I've said everything I needed to. Can we please go now?"

"Of course." She slides an arm around my shoulders.

"Renee," Krav snarls, tensing like he's about to lunge for me.

"She's staying with us now," Khan says firmly but calmly, inserting himself between us. "You should accept her decision." Now a dude I've never met before is giving advice on what I need to the guy I'm in love with. Talk about terrible taste in men.

I allow myself one last look at the demon who stole my heart, trying to memorize every detail of his face. His eyes are glittering, his mouth set in a rigid line. Everything in me aches to leap back through the swirling gateway and into his arms. I'm in a new and unfamiliar room, in Khan and Emma's palace, but if I concentrate, I can still smell Krav's whisky and bitter chocolate scent.

The edges of the portal flicker, blazing with a brilliant light before it collapses. The view of my bedroom—and Krav seething in the center of it—disappears.

"Come on, let's get you a drink," Emma murmurs, leading me away, her arm still curved around me. Khan stays close behind us, a silent, protective shield.

I wish I had one of those for my heart.

I wait until Emma has shown me to my new room, and she and Khan have left to give me space. Until the last trace of Krav's scent has faded. I fiddle with the clasp on my collar, pulling it off. I should toss it away, but can't bring myself to part with it so I stuff it under my pillow instead.

Only then do I lie back and, as the enormity of what I've just done sinks in, I finally allow the tears to come.

SIXTEEN

Krav

THEY SAY when an Alpha is separated from his Omega, the pain in the bond is unbearable. It aches like a missing limb, and will only lessen when they are reunited.

I'm striving to take all of it so none of it will touch her. Maybe it will increase the speed with which she forgets me, but I can't bear the thought of her feeling any of this anguish.

It burns like fire, so in an attempt to dull the agony with a different sort of burn, I fly to the point of utter exhaustion, until my wings are numb and frozen. When I return to my turret, I can barely fold them until I've thawed out by the fire, and even then it hurts.

She left me.

Desperate for relief, I make haste to my father's rooms and tear the lock off his desk to get at his stash of demon brew—the potent, bitter liquor he drank so often, especially towards the end of his life. The liquid burns down my throat and fills my stomach with lava, but I welcome the pain. It distracts me from the agony of our severed bond.

Mount Vracor is still rumbling. Awakened from its

slumber at last, it has come alive with a vengeance, spewing twice as much smoke and ash as before. Missives have been arriving from settlements all over Pyreda, the people pleading for me to do something. After glancing at the scrolls, I use them as extra fuel for the fire. I have no desire to see anyone ever again.

Nine jars of demon brew later, the orb on my desk flickers, and Khan's face appears. "Demon," he greets me.

"Wanderer." I don't bother to hide my contempt. "You are bold to contact me so soon after stealing from me."

"I wish to speak with you."

I could smash the orb but it would not harm him. And he would only appear in another one. "Return my Omega. That is all I have to say."

Khan scowls. "Renee is free to come to you any time she chooses."

Her name on another Alpha's lips is like needles in my spine. I thump down my cup. "Here's a question for you," I snarl. "How would you like it if our places were reversed? If my Omega convinced yours that she was not happy with you, that she should leave you, and then we helped her escape?"

Khan's expression is mutinous. "My queen—"

"Ah yes, your *queen*." I scoff. Khan's face turns an unhealthy shade of purple. "Does Emma always speak for you now? Do you no longer have a voice at all? Perhaps you should regain control of your own Hoo-man before you criticize how I'm handling mine."

Khan leans forward until his face fills the entire surface of the orb. His canines flash when he speaks. "I do not control Emma," he rasps. "I love her. I would die for her. I almost did. I would take your face off for daring to so much as say her name, but she has a kind heart. She wouldn't want me to harm you—for Renee's sake. But don't mistake my restraint for weakness. I don't have to put a collar and leash on my Omega as if she were some kind of animal and I feared she might run away. She is my queen. My mate. My equal. The mother of my children. When given the chance to return back to her planet, she chose to stay in Altrim with me even though she was afraid, confused, and homesick. Can you say your *pet* —" he spits the word with contempt, "—would do the same?"

I clench my fists, my claws shredding my palms.

"We already know the answer to that," Khan continues. "You made her so unhappy that she'd rather stay here with us than be with you."

Every word is like a poison-tipped dart piercing my chest. But the demon brew has made me slow. Sluggish. Unable to respond the way I want to.

"Our queens are the best things that ever happened to us," Khan goes on. "They are precious gifts, but powerful in their own right. Emma tells me Renee wanted to stay with you. She tried to *make it work*. But you would not accept her as an equal. If she is your mate, if you share a soul-bond, you should love her as she loves you."

I want to argue but I bite my tongue. I never told Renee how I felt about her because I didn't know. All my life, it's been drummed into me that demons are incapable of love. And whenever there were pangs of joy, belonging, or trust in my chest, I assumed they were her feelings, coming to me via the bond.

Only when she left me was I forced to face the truth: I do love her.

Khan is still staring at me. Shoving my sorrow aside, I summon back my anger. "Taking another's Omega is an act of war." I want to sound threatening, but the demon brew slurs my speech. "Beware, lest I make fire spill from Altrim's sky like rain."

"You can't. Your powers are too weak to extend to my

kingdom. Besides, you would not set Altrim alight while your Omega is here."

He's right. Damn him.

When Khan next speaks, to my astonishment, he sounds slightly bemused. "I would oblige you, and give you a fight. But battling me will not convince Renee to return to you. Why don't you fight to prove your love for her instead?"

With a low growl, I reach out and slap the orb to wipe his smug grin off its surface. But when his image has faded, his words echo in my ears.

Fight to prove your love for her.

The question is: how? I gave her everything I could, and it wasn't enough.

Ulf help me, I don't know what else to do.

I just know I cannot go on without her.

Renee

There's a baby in my lap, an adorably pudgy, roly-poly infant with lavender skin and sky-blue eyes. Emma and Khan's new son Kharon hasn't learned to crawl yet, but he's already great at blowing bubbles.

I duck my head and coo at him. "It's official," I announce to Emma, who's lounging on a nearby couch. "I'm in love. With you," I croon to Kharon. "With this gorgeous baby."

There's a touch of sadness to Emma's smile. She and I have discussed my rekindled desire to start family. At length, deep into the night. "You're always welcome to babysit."

"Anytime," I say, ignoring the flash of pain in my heart. Not in the bond. There's been no humming from the connection between me and Krav. No music. Nothing, not even a twinge of discomfort or regret. So much for soul-bonds.

It's been nice staying here with Emma and Khan, enjoying their breathtaking mountain palace. My room has an actual waterfall pouring past its balcony. And their kids are adorable. Emilia is old enough to run around and get into everything. She's off with a play group this morning.

I could imagine making a home here with Emma and her king and two littles. I'd be the best cool aunt. I might never have kids of my own but reading Emilia bedtime stories, holding Kharon and rocking him to sleep would be a good compromise.

Emma and I also discussed how I could return to Earth, but I shot that down real quick. What do I have to return for? My life there is over and the old Renee is gone. I like the new me better.

And, although I don't want to admit it, part of me hopes to reunite with Krav.

"You still have time," Emma says later, when Kharon's asleep and it's just us in her studio, day drinking like the *Real Housewives of Ulfaria*. Emma's introduced me to all kinds of local fermented juices, and I've become something of a mixologist. I have a bar in the corner of my bedroom, near the waterfall.

See? I could totally be the cool aunt.

"You're super fertile," Emma continues, because there's no such thing as TMI between us. She brought over a magician to check me out and answer my questions. I got confirmation that my baby factory is in excellent shape. Emma insists plenty of women have successful pregnancies in their forties, and I'm sure that's true, but the Omega serum would add an extra layer of reassurance.

"Yes, but the impregnation is only one part of the equation." I stretch out my arms. "My problem is the lack of a willing baby-daddy."

Emma sips her drink and hums. I don't like the gleam in her eye. She gets it when she's feeling extra mischievous.

"There are other kings, you know. The King Of Ruins has sent word to all the kingdoms, declaring his desire for an Omega. Khan showed me a picture of him—he's hot. Not as hot as Khan, but…"

"You don't think anyone is as hot as Khan," I say, mostly to tease and distract her.

She flushes. "True. But there are other sexy, single kings to choose from. And if you don't fancy being a queen, there are a boatload of other Alphas on Ulfaria. Most of them are soldiers, so you know they're fit…"

I twirl my glass. This cocktail has an infusion of *leeberries*. The taste reminds me of sitting in Krav's lap, eating pastries from his hand like his pampered pet… I shake myself. "What did you say that guy was king of? Ruins?"

"Ruins. He's also called the King of Ruses. Supposedly, his kingdom was destroyed in a *Chitin* attack. They're these alien bugs that attack Ulfaria from time to time–"

"You told me about them. I had nightmares afterwards. Giant bugs… ugh." I suppress a shudder.

"Anyway, instead of rebuilding, supposedly they left the ruins standing as a reminder to the people to always be on their guard. But Khan has a theory that they did rebuild their kingdom, and the real one is hidden under the ruins."

I rub the bridge of my nose. "Sounds confusing."

Emma chuckles. "Yeah. Regardless, like I said, the king is hot. Do you want to meet him? I'm sure he'd give you all the babies you want…"

But he's not Krav. "No thanks." I set my drink down and stop my hand from going to my neck, to rub the empty spot where my collar used to be. It's been days, and I miss its reassuring touch against my skin. I still sleep with it under my pillow.

I'm a mess.

It's gonna be okay. I can live here. I can be the cool aunt. When life give you lemons... "Margaritas," I mumble.

"What?"

I look up. Emma's studio also has a waterfall cascading down the rock face beyond the seating area, and she's pretending to admire it. She's great at giving me space. She may not be seven feet tall with a deviant tail but at least she has empathy.

"Margaritas." I pick up my glass and examine it, holding my breath so I don't get a whiff of the *leeberries*. "I think I'll try margaritas next."

"Sounds yummy," Emma says. "You have one day to perfect the recipe. We're having a girls' night tomorrow."

"Aren't all our nights girls' nights?" I've been worried about keeping her up too late. She's still nursing the baby, and Emilia wakes up at the crack of dawn. I don't want to monopolize her time, but she seems happy to hang out with me. Khan's been busy, away a lot. He takes an active role in ruling his kingdom.

Unlike some people I know.

"Tomorrow is special," Emma says. "I've invited the other queens over."

I sit up so fast, my drink sloshes. "You did?" We've talked about them so much I feel like I already know them, but I haven't gotten to meet them yet.

"Yep. Kim is dying for a girls' night now that baby Auryn is comfortable with a bottle. I haven't heard back from the others yet, but Kim will definitely be here."

"Awesome!"

The huge stone doors glide open and Khan prowls in. He's taller and leaner than most other Alphas I've seen—and I've seen several since I got here, he has an entire army—but he has an air of power about him. A commanding presence. He favors simple clothes but you could pick him out of a crowd and know he was in charge.

He says nothing, but strides over to Emma and leans down. It's my turn to pretend to study the waterfall as they embrace. If only I could put my hands over my ears and block out the loving murmurs and smacking sounds.

After what feels like forever, the imposing Alpha straightens and gives me a nod. "Greetings."

"Hi."

Emma has gone limp in her seat, a dreamy look on her face. "I thought you'd be out all day." Khan owns fleets of spaceships with which he supplies Ulfaria, and trades on their behalf.

"I just returned—and found the loading dock filled with these." He waves a hand and a floating platform—Emma tells me they're called skimmers—drifts towards us. It's piled high with boxes and bulky, cloth-covered shapes. "Delivered today for Renee... from Pyreda."

"What? For me?" I rise and the platform floats to me, stopping a foot away. "What is this stuff?" A glossy fur in a shimmery shade of purple spills over the edge. "Krav sent this?"

"That would be my guess." Khan folds his arms, glowering at the gifts as if their presence offends him.

"Oooh, presents!" Emma claps her hands. "What did you get?"

I touch one box and it opens with a whoosh of magic. Inside is a carefully folded gown. I hold it up.

"Stunning colors," Emma says. "It'll look gorgeous on you."

"Maybe." I put it back. It's a simple style—a warm day dress in shimmering rainbow tones. Mystic topaz, like Krav's eyes.

I touch each box and peek at the contents.

"Is it all clothes?" Emma asks.

"Some blankets. Some pillows. More clothes."

"He seems to believe we would not give you the barest hospitality!" Khan folds his arms over his chest. I revise my earlier observation—he has plenty of muscled bulk.

Emma places a hand on his bulging, lilac bicep. "I'm sure he just misses her."

"Yeah," I say. "He… used to make all my clothes for me." And the soft furnishings I needed for my bedroom when I was nesting. A mat so I could do yoga. He even managed permanent mascara. I gaze at the boxes overflowing with warm clothes, blankets, pillows—he wants to make sure I'm comfortable. I resist the temptation to bury my cold hands in the furs.

"That's… kind of sweet," Emma says.

The smallest box contains a couple of *leeberry* tarts and a few *kiktu* fruits. There's even a flagon of *hima* juice. All my favorites.

He's trying. Maybe I was too hasty in leaving. Maybe he's changed.

Or maybe that's what I want to think because I miss him.

He sent food, drink, clothing, bedding… Exactly what you'd give a pet. "Nice try," I mutter. What might he send me next? The leash I left behind? Maybe a crate, like I'm a cat he's taking to the vet.

I realize I'm holding my neck and drop my hand. "He's tried all this before. Same shit, different day… it means nothing." Hardening my resolve, I set about closing up the boxes. "Do you want any of these fur cloaks, Emma? They're really nice. And cruelty free." I shake one out to show her, and something clinks to the floor. It's a small stone object. I toss it back on the pile. Every part of me longs to fold myself into the sumptuous fabric and drink in his scent, so I stuff the cloak deep into a nearby box.

"Even if you don't want them, they're your gifts," Emma says.

I huff and turn to Khan. "Can you send all this stuff back?"

He grimaces. "The Demon King would take offence, and accuse me of not delivering the gifts properly."

Goddamnit.

"I'll have them sent to your room," Khan continues, and I narrow my eyes at him. Sometimes I wonder if he's on Krav's side. "If the demon asks, I will tell him the gifts were delivered, but nothing more."

"Thank you." It's a compromise, I guess. But I hate the thought of the items in my room, smelling like him, a constant reminder…

"Now, if you'll excuse us, I need a private word with my mate." He turns to Emma, his hand sliding possessively around the nape of her neck. Emma sucks in a breath, drinking in his scent. Her eyelashes flutter. Khan smells nice, but not delicious. Not like my favorite blend of smoky whisky and chocolate.

"Of course," I say, scurrying for the door. Khan's been away a lot lately but it's clear he's going to make up for it today.

It's okay; I'm happy for Emma. At least one of us is getting sexed up by her Alpha.

Not that I'm missing mine. It's just that he gave me the best orgasms of my life…

I turn down the hall and slow my steps. The platform full of gifts floats just behind me, following me to my room. I'm careful to stay in front of it, avoiding Krav's scent.

Maybe I do miss more than the orgasms.

But it doesn't matter how much I miss him. What I told Emma was the truth: Krav sending me these gifts doesn't make a difference. This is not new proof he's grown capable of love. Possessions are his thing, and he always gave me anything I wanted—for my material comfort.

Nothing's changed, and as things stand, being with him would break my heart. Unrequited love is the worst, and not even the best sex in the world can make up for it.

That's what I tell myself when I lie awake at night. Forgiving Krav and moving back to Pyreda would just mean dooming myself to a shallow relationship without the love and respect I crave from him. The hollow ache of sleeping alone. The uncertainty of how he'll react when I ask him questions he doesn't like. The frustration of watching him follow in his father's footsteps when his kingdom—his *people* —deserve so much more.

I don't want any part of that. The old Renee might have stayed and tried to make things work, sacrificing herself and her needs for too long, but I've come a long way since then.

Going through my divorce was one of the hardest things I've ever done, but at least it taught me self-respect. That you need to teach people how to treat you. And if they don't want to learn, you GTFO.

The only option I have is to stay busy so I don't think of him. Luckily, I have a girls' night to prepare for. After all, the margaritas ain't gonna mix themselves.

SEVENTEEN

AFTER AN ENTIRE DAY of waiting to hear back from Altrim, I reach out to Khan. He made it clear Renee has no desire to see me, but he cannot decline my calls forever, so I will keep trying regardless of how much it annoys him.

As far as I'm concerned, annoying him is a bonus.

I press the button, the orb pulses with light, and the Wanderer's grumpy face appears. "What is it now?"

"Did she receive the gifts?"

"Yes."

"What did she think of them?"

"If she wanted you to know, she'd tell you herself."

If I punch the orb, it will shatter. Khan would remain unscathed. Still, it would be satisfying.

Not as satisfying as flying to Altrim and ripping the guts out of their space-faring ships. How powerful would the Wanderer King be without his armada of flying vessels?

But I will not compromise the safety of my Omega. Should the *Chitin*—or anyone else—attack, Khan would need his ships to protect his kingdom.

Nothing matters, as long as Renee is safe. She may have left me, but she's constantly foremost in my thoughts.

"Demon, your gifts are not necessary." Khan sounds irritated. "We are providing Renee with everything she needs. Did you think we would not?"

My tail thumps the rug behind my chair. Of course I assumed Khan would provide basic hospitality—food and shelter—for Renee. But he and his queen do not know my Omega like I do. They don't know how cold her hands get. How she presses them to my chest to warm them. That she adores *hima* juice. Altrim has a temperate clime, not prone to extremes like Pyreda, but still… "She is fragile," I insist. *She is precious.*

"She can also take care of herself."

She has no need to. That's what I am here for.

Except she left me, and I can take care of her no more.

Khan sighs. "Do you want my advice?"

"No."

"Then end this call, because I'm going to give it anyway." I'm about to reach for the orb when the next thing he says is, "Your Omega misses you." I stay my hand.

There's an infuriating smirk on Khan's face. He knows he has my attention.

"She longs to return to your side," he says. "She is lonely here without you. But you won't get her back unless she sees that things are different. You need to show her that you care for her."

I clench my fists. He said this the last time we spoke, and I tried, but it didn't work. I don't know what else I could do. "How?"

"By taking care of her heart and soul, as well as her body. Give her what she *needs*. Not what you think she wants. Now if you'll excuse me, my queen is waiting for me. Unlike you, I know what *my* mate both wants *and* needs." He ends the connection before I can smash the orb to pieces.

Overcome with rage, I rise from my chair, my wings billowing behind me. I flap them furiously, venting, knocking over ornaments and furniture, making the ash from the fireplace swirl through the air.

Chest heaving, heart pounding, I survey the maelstrom of chaos I wrought in my own room. I'm throwing a tantrum, like I often did when I was young.

Sadly, I no longer have my mother here to guide me.

Do not show weakness, my father would say. *Always maintain the upper hand. The Omega left because you were too kind to her. You coddled her. She didn't fear you enough. Didn't respect the boundaries.* He would endorse my rage.

But my mother? She was always sad. My father—her mate—treated her coldly, keeping her at a distance. I never saw them embrace or exchange smiles. My mother spent most of her time hiding in her rooms, playing her beloved *hriox,* plucking out the melodic tunes from her homeland. And sometimes she played tragic love ballads. The tortured notes sounded like a weeping female.

It is the same agonized sound that wails in my bond.

I have no doubt that she would have wanted more for herself than a cruel mate who refused to treat her kindly. Who saw her as inferior. Who refused to love her.

And she would have wanted more for her son.

My father taught me to remain cold and stoic. To rule with fear. He said it was the demon way—that since we are forged by fire, we are superior beings. Strong. Fearless.

Maybe it was not the demon way. Maybe it was *his* way. Renee was right. My father was an Ulfdamn asshole. And I may be strong but I am no longer fearless.

I did not know true terror until I saw my Omega step through the portal—and my greatest fear was realized. Perhaps that's why my sire was so adamant about keeping his mate at arm's length even after she bore him a child. Maybe he treated my mother the way he did because he knew that to love someone is to risk losing them... to *fear* losing them.

I rise and pace to the window. Mount Vracor is smoking again. Its rumbles have died down, but I can sense the turmoil within. The village elders are inundating me with missives, begging me to do something about it.

The beads in my beard click as I stroke the braids. It helps me think.

All my life, I strove to be like my father, and what was the result? A neglected kingdom and an anguished Omega. I grew up watching my mother suffer, furious that I was helpless to stop it. I can't believe I almost condemned my own mate to the same fate.

The snow is still falling. It coats the mountains and hills. Even the edges of the lava lake sparkle with lavender crystals.

The memory of Renee's reaction to the snow makes me smile. Her enthusiasm was infectious, whether she was talking about Hoo-man customs, or admiring something she found pretty. What did she say? *The snow is beautiful. You don't think your kingdom is beautiful?*

My Omega saw the best in my kingdom. She saw the best in me.

Maybe it's time I lived up to the version of myself she— and my mother—believed in.

Renee

One hour into girls' night and my cheeks ache from grinning so much. I couldn't figure out a good Ulfarri dupe for tequila, so the margaritas aren't quite right, but they're still a big hit. Especially with Kim, who's another pint-sized blonde. What she lacks in height, she makes up for in personality. I've never seen anyone so energetic.

Right now, she's shadowboxing, glass in hand. "Girls!" She swigs her drink and performs a high kick. "Who runs this motherfucka?"

"We do!" Emma and I chorus back from our places on the couch.

"Then drink!"

I take a sip of my margarita. Emma, caught up in the excitement, takes a huge gulp and chokes.

"Whew, that's strong," she sputters, and I pat her on the back. "I'm okay. It was just a lot to swallow."

"That's what she said!" Kim cries. The girl has two volumes: loud, and extra loud.

"What's this flavor again?" Emma asks me with a hiccup.

"*Hima,* but I added some *kiktu* for the tang."

Emma licks her lips. "It's good stuff."

Kim agrees, collapsing on a couch opposite us. "So I have a question," she says, then lets out a burp. "Excuse me."

"You're excused."

"Thanks. That wasn't my question." She points at me. "You, Rose, and Haley got Omega-ized by the same group of rogue magicians. How did you all end up in different kingdoms, and at different times?"

"Rose and Haley arrived around the same time," Emma corrects. "But Rose had already been here for months by the time we heard about her—"

"Yeah, yeah. But you," Kim points at me with her glass, "show up now. What is that, like two years later? Three?"

I shrug. I have no idea.

"Stasis?" Emma suggests. "They could've been put in stasis pods and dumped at different times. To avoid an influx of Omegas?"

"Don't look at me," I say. "I know less about all this stuff than either of you, and I can't remember anything that happened before I woke up. Still, better late than never, I guess?"

"I'll drink to that." Kim toasts me. "All's well that ends well, right?"

"Exactly," I say.

"We can ask Rose and Haley what they think at the next girls' night. Where are they, anyway?" Kim asks.

"Rose sends her apologies. She's busy with affairs of state," Emma says.

"Girl boss," Kim crows.

"Good for her," I add. Rose sounds badass.

"And Haley never RSVP'd. She's probably gone off the grid with her Alpha again. They're all about nature, and like to disappear for weeks at a time. You know, living off the land," Emma explains to me.

"Yeah, they love that life." Kim wanders over to the bar to top up her drink. "Word is they've got a sweet sex cave."

"You have a one-track mind," Emma says.

"And I'm proud of it. But anyway, speaking of couples' secrets… I want to hear about Renee's guy."

"Since we recently broke up, there's not much to say," I mutter.

Beside the bar floats the skimmer, still piled high with the gifts Krav sent me. The only things I touched were the flagon of *hima* juice and the *kiktu*—for the cocktails. Kim pauses to peer at the boxes. "You didn't want any of these things?"

"Nope. It's all just more of the same. I want evidence he's *changed*." Emma and Kim both blink at me, so I explain, "He used to give me stuff like that all the time. Gifts. Called me his *pet*… and treated me like one."

"Hey, if you're into that kind of thing, I don't judge," Kim says.

I manage a smile. "To be fair, I was into it, but then I fell for him and—"

"And she wanted him to love her back," Emma finishes for me when my voice cracks.

"Wait—he doesn't love you?" Kim's eyebrows are almost touching her hairline.

I swallow past the lump in my throat. "He believes demons aren't capable of love," I tell her. "Seems like he's determined to take after his asshole dad in that regard. So while he took care of every aspect of my physical well-being, he always kept me at a distance emotionally. Like there was an invisible barrier between us. He never listened to what I was telling him, never showed any interest in me as a person." I sigh. "He doesn't care about his people, either— says they should be strong enough to fend for themselves. I think that's what gets to me the most."

There's no point in mentioning Mount Vracor. It's not like Emma or Kim can do anything to help. Besides, this subject is depressing and we're meant to be having fun.

"What is this supposed to be? A toy?" Kim holds up the little object I rescued when it dropped out from the folds of the cloak.

I take it, examining it closely for the first time. It's a piece of stone like obsidian, carved into a tiny shape.

"Is that a mini statue of Krav?" Kim asks. "It's got wings. You said he has wings, right?"

"Yeah, but this isn't him." I hold it up and point out the claw feet and lion's body, topped with the eagle-like head. "It's a *styxian*. They're like griffins. Krav keeps one as a pet— he's called Plutus."

I marvel at the delicate carving and the thought behind this gift. Krav sent me a miniature Plutus, a figurine of his beloved pet—whom he cared for against his father's wishes. Proof that Krav wasn't his father, that he had a softer side. I miss that part of him.

I also miss his intensity. The fiery heat of his lust, the cool composure of his control. The way he'd dominate me until my orgasms flayed me open. The way he'd gather my hands to his chest to warm them.

Tears fill my eyes. "Oh, guys." I rest my hand on my throat, mimicking the weight of the collar I used to wear, and surreptitiously stroke the scar where Krav claimed me. Whenever my heart threatens to burst from the pain, touching the bite mark soothes me. "I want to see him again."

"No," Kim and Emma say in unison.

"I know it's a bad idea—"

"Do not, and I cannot repeat this enough, *do not* call your ex." Kim lifts her glass in my direction, sloshing it all over herself.

"Stop." Emma grabs her arm, which only makes the drink spill more. "Kim! You're spraying everywhere."

"That's what she said," Kim says with a wink, and they both dissolve into giggles.

"Guys, I'm serious. I wonder… would there be a way to see him but without him seeing me?"

"Like a spy cam?" Kim guzzles the rest of her drink and sets the empty glass down. "I'm sure we can rig that. Rose told me her guy has them all over his palace."

"Creepy." Emma hands Kim a wet cloth, and Kim mops the spilled drink off her face, cleavage and hands..

"Eh, exhibitionism and voyeurism are valid kinks," Kim says. "Not my preference, but if they enjoy it…"

Emma shoots me a look. She and I had a long conversation about BDSM and our submissive sides. She used to go to clubs to get her fix. We both have a working theory that the Omega serum works in tandem with our masochistic streaks and love of power play, somehow enhancing them.

I suspect Kim has her own ideas about that, but right now she's busy setting up an orb in front of me and fiddling with it.

It takes less time than I thought it would to rig one of the orbs to give me a live visual of Krav. Kim assures me it's a one-way view—I can see him, but he can't see me. The sphere pulses with light and I peer into its milky depths, my two new friends behind me.

I'm holding my breath as if waiting for a blow. I expect to see Krav in his castle chambers, lounging by the fire with his wings akimbo and a bored expression on his face. A still life painting titled: *Demon King Enjoys His Solitude*.

The image comes into focus... and there he is. My heart skips at the sight of him. He is on a throne, but it doesn't look like he's in his castle. His spine is straight, his posture regal. Glittering gold and silver strands are draped over his horns.

He's wearing a gold and red robe trimmed with black fur. Someone is bowing to him.

"Where is he?" I whisper. Now that I'm doing it, I feel kinda guilty about spying on him but I can't tear my eyes away.

The camera pans out to reveal the whole scene. Krav sits on a throne in the middle of a village square with people thronging around him. A familiar crimson figure with bright orange hair stands beside the throne, wringing his hands. It's Alkarvi, the village elder who took one look at me and decided I'd make a good sacrificial virgin.

"The heck is going on over—" Kim begins but I hold up a hand to stop her.

"Is there sound?" I ask.

Reaching over my shoulder, Kim does something to the orb. "There should be... there we go."

"Hear, ye, hear ye! His Evilness is ready for another supplicant!" Alkarvi announces.

Krav beckons him with a claw, and the two put their heads together to confer. I strain but can't hear what they're saying. After a moment, Alkarvi straightens up and clears his throat.

"Excuse me. The king *formerly* known as His Evilness is ready for another supplicant. You may call him *Satan*!"

Krav lets out a huge sigh and beckons Alkarvi to him again. There's another whispered conference, followed by a new announcement.

"Not Satan! *Santa!*"

Krav rolls his eyes but he looks more bemused than anything else.

Alkarvi gestures to a short, pink-skinned Ulfarri, beckoning him forward. "Come, child! Make your request to Santa."

"I wish for my fangs to finally come in," the little one squeaks. "And… I want a *tyrlee!*"

Krav bows his head so he's at eye-level with the kid. The gold and silver strands adorning his horns glint in the suns' light as he moves.

I'm holding my breath, half-expecting the Demon King to bellow in the little one's face. But Krav's voice is calm—jovial, even. "Have you been behaving yourself? Doing what your mother and father tell you?"

The kid drags his toes across the ground. "Mostly, Your Evi—Santa."

"Mostly is a good start," Krav says. "Mind that you continue to be good for your parents. As for your wishes… your fangs will descend in time and grow bigger at the same rate as the rest of you." He reaches beside his throne before handing the child a cup and a small plate piled high with what look like *leeberry* tarts. "You will drink this white juice and eat these *koo-keys* to get big and strong." The kid accepts the gifts carefully, grinning over his shoulder at two taller Ulfarri with similar markings who are probably his parents.

Sitting up tall, Krav roars, "Bring forth the *tyrlee!*"

"I don't understand…" I blink several times and even give my wrist a pinch, but the strange scene in the orb remains the same. "Krav was adamant that he never visited the villages, let alone handed out gifts to people."

"It looks like some kind of local ritual," Emma says. "See there? They're putting up decorations."

I lean closer. The Pyredii who aren't queueing to see Krav are bustling about, nailing bunches of silver and gold threads to their doorjambs. One is swaying on a rickety ladder, fastening a bright red bunch of leaves to the frame of his hut.

"Ahhh. I think I know what's happening," Kim says. "Earlier today, Aurus was asking me a bunch of stuff about *Hoo-man holidays*, particularly Christmas. I asked why he wanted to know, and he told me it was *official business*. I bet Krav called him."

None of this makes sense. Krav's too proud and arrogant to admit he doesn't know something. Besides, he'd never ask anyone for help or advice, let alone another Alpha. And even if he did, why the heck would he want to know more about Christmas? He didn't seem *that* interested when I tried to describe it. "What did you tell him?"

"I tried to explain that there were lots of different human holidays, and different ways to celebrate Christmas. But he insisted on more details, so I told him how we always did it in our family." Kim ticks items off on her fingers as she lists them. "Gift giving, Santa Claus, Rudolph the red-nosed reindeer. All that stuff."

"Look." Emma points. "That *tyrlee* has a red nose!"

Alkarvi has abandoned his post beside Krav to clip a leash on a weird-looking creature—like a cross between a cow and a horse—and lead it out of its pen. There's a dab of glossy crimson paint on the animal's nose.

"Accept this gift from Santa," Krav announces, placing the end of the leash in the kid's hand. "And let it be known that demons make benevolent and generous kings!"

The crowd cheers, and the child leads his new pet away. His parents wave their hands in the air, looking ecstatic.

"The next petitioner to the King Santa may approach!" Alkarvi calls out.

Another kid dashes forward, beads rattling in her hair. "Can I ride the monster?" she squeaks, pointing to the sky where Plutus is dipping and wheeling in the distance. The adult behind the little girl gasps and clutches her chest.

"Alas, you cannot," Krav tells her. "He bites. But look..." He flips his hand in a shower of sparks and a little figurine of the *styxian* appears between his talons. It looks similar to the one he gave me. The kid lets out a gasp of delight.

"What do you say?" her mother prompts behind her.

"Thank you, Your Evilness! May you rule in darkness and torment forever."

"You are most welcome." Krav snaps his fingers to get Alkarvi's attention. "Give this one a *tyrlee* as well. And, little one, don't forget your white juice and *koo-keys*." The child toddles along behind Alkarvi, juggling the cup of what I assume contains *white juice*, and a plate of tarts.

I glance over my shoulder at Kim. "White juice?"

She shrugs. "Maybe the closest thing on Ulfaria to our milk back home? I told Aurus about the milk and cookie tradition. He must have gotten it mixed up, because the kids are getting them, not leaving them out."

"And Krav's playing Santa," Emma says. "Look, he's in red and... um, black. With... tinsel on his horns. I mean, he looks kind of like a Santa."

"From hell," Kim adds.

A Santa from hell. Beyond Krav's throne, a few of the villagers are hoisting up a giant, twisted tree with a blackened trunk and branches. Once they've secured it, the children rush to decorate the lower boughs with silver and gold strands—their idea of tinsel—and tiny carvings of Plutus spinning on thread.

"This is because of me." My hand slides to my neck. "Because of the snow."

Emma and Kim give me puzzled looks.

"It was snowing, and I got so excited. I told him all about

Christmas, and other holiday traditions. He must have been paying attention after all." At least enough to get the gist, and then ask Aurus to pump Kim for more details.

"And now he's recreating it," Emma says. "But why?"

"That's the million-dollar question. I don't have a freaking clue." I wish I did.

My mind whirling, I sink back into the couch. Just seeing Krav made me ache with longing—hearing his voice was excruciating. The way he spoke to those kids... the fact that he was there in the first place, giving his people gifts instead of terrorizing them...

Why recreate Christmas? It couldn't be for my benefit—he didn't know I was watching.

"You can turn it off," I tell Kim, gesturing to the orb. "Thanks so much for making that happen."

"Anytime. Remind me to show you how to do it before I leave. You know, just in case you want to... check in again."

"I appreciate that," I say. "So much."

"It makes a nice change to see you smiling," Emma says.

"Now we know: all it takes to make her happy is a shitload of margaritas and a spy cam," Kim adds with a grin.

"Shuddurp, you two," I pretend to scold them. But for the first time since I stepped through the portal, the bond is humming a faint but sweet melody.

And there's a flicker of something in my chest that I didn't expect to feel again anytime soon.

Hope.

EIGHTEEN

Krav

I USED to think all settlements in Pyreda looked the same. From above, they all consist of huts around a village square. But in my quest to bring Renee's Hoo-man holiday joy to my kingdom, I have become familiar with the unique features of each one.

This settlement is a long way from my castle but close to Mount Vracor. Above us, the volcano spews thick smoke into the frosty air. The earthquakes are more frequent—a bad sign. I've spent hours flying around it, searching for a way to quench the raging inferno in its core. But while I can feel the volcano's turmoil, I'm not strong enough to soothe it. I can only plan and prepare for the day when it erupts.

In the meantime, I have a mission to fulfil.

It's strangely rewarding to be welcomed joyfully by my people. They surge around my throne until I order elders to press them back. Children and their parents form a queue, and I beckon the first eager family forward to give them their gifts.

One by one, I grant wishes, gratified by the smiles I'm

putting on bright young faces. It reminds me of the way my pet would beam whenever she found something especially pleasing.

What I wouldn't give to be the reason she smiles again.

The suns are high overhead, blazing through the haze of smoke, when a hush falls over the crowd. Out of nowhere, there's a shower of gold sparks, and the parents closest to it snatch their children out of the way. The air between the sparks grows opaque until it shimmers and solidifies.

It's a portal.

I rise, my wings snapping to their full span. The last time such a gateway opened in my kingdom, Renee disappeared through it, and my world was shattered.

My heart is thudding as I wait, my fists clenched, inundated with memories of that awful day. But instead of Renee stepping through the golden circle to a palace in Altrim, she is stepping out, daintily holding up the hem of her gown so she doesn't trip on the rocky ground.

The villagers murmur, keeping their distance but craning their heads to see the spectacle. Renee straightens up, her fire-stone hair glinting in the light of the suns, and the Pyredii gasp as if she's the most beautiful thing they've ever seen.

She is the most beautiful thing I've ever seen.

I dare not move or speak, lest this is a dream. The bond in my chest hums.

Renee picks her way delicately over to the throne, beaming at me, her smile like sunlight I don't deserve.

"Hello," she calls in her musical voice.

I want to say, *Hello, my pet,* but her bare neck is a stark reminder that she is mine no longer. She looks healthy, her cheeks flushed and her green eyes sparkling.

"Renee." *You're here. Tell me you're real.* I clear my throat. "Is this a dream?"

"No. I'm really here. I've been watching you. For days

now. When I first saw what you were doing, I thought you were just blessing the people of Solum—the ones who found me and gifted me to you. But I kept watching, and saw you go to every village in Pyreda. Day in, day out, you were there, granting requests and spreading joy. I believe this is the last one?"

"It is."

"You gave them all Christmas!" She bites her lip. "I guess I just wanted to know… why?"

"Because speaking of this holiday gave you such joy. You have such happy memories of it, your face lit up when you described it to me. I wanted to give the Pyredii the same experience… what did you call it?"

"Holiday cheer?" she whispers.

"Yes."

She's gazing up at me, her eyes full of emotion. Even more freckles are sprinkled over her cheekbones and across her nose. I want to look at her for hours and count them all.

I force myself to continue, "They enjoy the gifts. And the *jynx* infused the white juice with essential nutrients that's good for the little ones' growth." I raise my voice, addressing the gathered crowd. "For too long, I have been a neglectful ruler. My father taught me that demons should rule through fear. But he was wrong. The Omega Renee showed me the truth. There is a better way."

The people cheer, but all my attention has returned to the little Hoo-man in front of me.

"Krav," she whispers.

"I was wrong," I tell her. "I'll never forgive myself for how I treated you. While I cannot go back and change that, I have resolved to be a good king in future, as you admonished."

"You're doing well." She casts an admiring look around, but still does not move closer or touch me. Her scent wafts my way, making me dizzy.

"I had hoped to one day see you again. But I did not dare

to dream it would be so soon." I give in to my longing and lift a finger to her cheek, caressing her smooth skin where the pink of her blush blends with the amber constellation of markings. "You are beautiful, as always."

She curves her mouth into a smile but her lower lip wobbles. "You always know what to say. I missed you."

"I missed you, too. So, so much." I can no longer hold back my tail. It slides around her leg, gripping her ankle under her skirt. "Have you been well?"

"Not really. Not until I looked into an orb and saw you. Saw this." She gestures to the throne, the decorations, and the citizens waiting in line. "And I came to help. I even dressed the part!" She gives a little twirl, making the fur hem of her red gown spin. Her outfit matches mine perfectly. "That is, if you'll have me?"

There's a rock in my throat, straining my voice. "Of course." Ensuring my talons are retracted, I hold out my hand. After a moment, she takes it. Hope spears my chest.

Renee came back to help me. I've being given another chance. Her slender fingers in my palm feel like home.

"But I must disagree with you on one thing," I tell her. "I do *not* always know what to say."

"No?" Her expression is wary.

"No. I've done a lot of thinking since you… since you left." I take a deep breath. "There are things I should have told you that I did not—"

"I know," she interrupts. "That you were using your magic to stop—"

"No—well, yes, that," I say hurriedly, "but also something else."

"Oh god. Is it a bad thing?"

An image of my father's face flashes in my mind's eye. "No. I don't think so. In fact, as far as I'm concerned, it's a wonderful thing."

Her green eyes are huge. Pools of emotion threatening to

drown me. "Well go on, don't keep me in suspense," she says.

"I love you."

Renee's free hand goes to her trembling lips. A fat tear escapes her lower lashes and trickles down her freckled cheek. I can't breathe.

"Have I upset you?" I whisper.

"No!" A second tear spills down her other cheek and she dashes it away. "No, you haven't upset me, you dumbass! Not if you mean it! Do you really mean it?"

"I do. I was a fool for not realizing it sooner, but Ulf knows it hit me when you disappeared through that portal. I love you so, so much. You're my mate. My life is empty and shallow without you in it. *I'm* empty and shallow without you—"

Her lips on mine cut off my speech and with a growl, I pull her up against me and kiss her with all the passion overflowing in my heart.

My Omega has returned to my side. A rush of relief and satisfaction threatens to topple me. Deep in my chest, the bond blasts open with a chorus of notes so loud, I expect the entire village to hear it.

When she finally pulls away, Renee's panting like she ran all the way to the top of a mountain. "Do you hear that?"

My entire being is filled by the intense music in the bond between us. "I do."

"Sounds like an angel choir," she murmurs, and laughs.

I cock my head to the side. I could stand here and listen and stare at her forever. Around us, the villagers wait patiently for the return of their Santa.

It's the perfect time to present my mate with her gift.

"I have something for you. If you'll accept it." I extend my free hand and a swirl of silvery light takes form, solidifying into a crown. It has five prongs in an identical black shade to my horns, and a giant golden fire-stone streaked with red glistens in the center of it.

Renee's breath *whooshes* out of her.

"I can make it rose-gold, if you like." My palm tingles and the crown quivers. The gleaming metal at the base turns pink and the color rises, gradually swallowing the black. "If you decide to stay with me—even for a moment or a single day—you will stand beside me not as my pet, but as my mate. My queen. My equal."

She reaches out to touch the crown, then hesitates. My blood freezes in the time it takes for her to blink and nod. "Yes. I accept."

"You do?"

She reaches for my wrist, wrapping her fingers around it as far as they'll go. "Of course I do! I love you! But…" she tugs me close, "I think I want to be more than just your queen."

"You are. You're my mate. My every—"

"Hush," she murmurs, cutting off my reassurances. "What I'm trying to say is," she reaches into her bodice and draws out the collar I gave her, "I kept this. I couldn't part with it. Will you put it back on me… Master? Please?"

My grin is so broad, my cheeks ache. I've never known such joy. "Yes, my pet. If you will wear your crown."

"I think I can do that." She bows her head, and I place the coronet in her gleaming hair.

Taking her gently by the shoulders, I turn her to face the crowd. "All hail, Queen Renee of Pyreda!" I announce.

The village elder takes up the call, and the crowd joins in. "All hail, Queen Renee!"

"Thank you." Renee slides a hand to the base of her bare throat. Her fingers creep up to stroke the mark I put on her, binding her to me. "I'm all good," she calls, and the portal, which I'd completely forgotten about, blinks out of existence.

She really is staying. Ulf be praised.

Renee looks up at me from under her lashes. "Now the collar," she whispers.

With careful fingers, I secure it around her neck.

A distant rumble warns of the coming earthquake. "Brace yourselves," I command everyone, summoning the *jynx* as the ground begins to tremble. I scoop up Renee before she's knocked off her feet. Behind us, the throne rocks on its platform. People cry out, clutching each other to stay upright. In their pen, the *tyrlee* bellow in distress and stamp their hooves. A few are rushing the fences, trying to get out. Plutus dips and wheels overhead, letting out an ear-splitting screech.

"Into the huts!" the elder cries. The festival tree, which the villagers spent hours erecting and decorating to my specifications, sways and crashes to the ground.

"No!" I shout. The *jynx* have prepared for this—it's why I summoned them immediately. "We will evacuate." I raise a hand and create a portal of my own with a shower of circling sparks. It leads to a great room in the lower floor of my castle. The *jynx* flit to and fro, herding people towards it, and guiding them through it with the help of the village elder.

Mount Vracor roars. The smoke billowing from its summit is as black as my horns.

I hoist Renee up higher against my chest. "I must get you to safety."

"We need to do something," she cries, coughing from the ash filling the air.

With a great leap, I launch us both into the sky. Renee presses her face against my chest, still wheezing.

I strain my wings, gaining height. Plutus flies with us, following just behind. I would shout at him to go, but he will not leave my side.

Renee clings to me. I've found a plume of fresh air, high above the village, but more and more smoke is escaping from Mount Vracor. Soon, everything will be swallowed by smoke and ash and fire.

While my Omega has returned to me, she cannot live in this land. Not like this. No one can.

But maybe it doesn't have to be like this.

I clutch my mate tight and head towards the volcano, into the eye of the storm. I can sense the borders of my kingdom, and Mount Vracor pulsing like a beating heart in the center. *Heart of the demon.* Summoning all my power, I strain to contain it but the fiery fury has been building for too long. It's too strong. If only there were two of me, combining our powers to halt the raging, destructive fires threatening to burst forth…

You are not meant to rule alone.

And I am not alone. I have my queen.

"Renee. My love." I squeeze her. "I need you."

She gazes up at me and blinks, her eyes streaming from the smoky air. "What do you need?"

"I need your help. My queen. My power alone is not enough to stop the volcano from erupting. But if you join me, if we combine our powers… we might stand a chance."

"Let's give it a shot." She coughs against my shoulder. "Tell me what to do."

I flap my wings, taking us closer. "Be still," I command her. "Listen to the music of the bond." I tune into the humming melody. It's been sweet since the moment Renee emerged from the portal and returned to my side.

No, that's not true. That was the moment it began to gain momentum. It's been humming happily since the day I began to bring the joy of Renee's holiday to my people. And it's underscored by the slower, deeper but no less harmonious music of the land.

"Can you hear it?" I ask Renee.

"Yes."

"Join me. Open your heart, and share the music of our bond with the land. Our union will heal it."

Renee closes her eyes, her long lashes fanning over her freckled face. "I feel it," she murmurs. "It's gorgeous… like a symphony."

I hear a thousand *hrioxes* playing my mother's favorite song—a ballad of her village, about a young man who goes away to find himself, only to return and realize his lover's arms is where he feels most at home.

Renee is humming something under her breath. "Let it snow…"

Ahead of us, Plutus squawks and wheels to the left. A vast plume of fire shoots out of the top of Mount Vracor. Sparks shower the thick black smoke.

Lava sprays into the sky. The summit's a dark cauldron, bubbling over. Molten rock, glowing with heat, oozes down the volcano's sides.

I pull up short, retreating before the scorching heat envelops us. "It's not working," I shout over the cacophony of the dying land. "We must go back."

Were I alone here, I would remain, fighting to my last breath to save Pyreda and my people. But I cannot bear to expose my mate to one more moment of danger. Every cell in my body is screaming at me to get her to safety immediately. To protect her.

"No! We can do this, I know we can! We just need to trust!" Renee arches her head up and seals her lips over mine. Sublime music swells in the bond, drowning out the crackles and rumbles all around us.

My heart surges, overflowing. My queen presses herself against me as if she intends to climb inside my chest. She's giving everything to the kiss—her heart. Her soul. Her love. Her moans. All echoing in the bond, each one a cord binding us closer.

I can give no less. I lean over her, breathing her in, plundering her sweet mouth with my tongue. She yields to me with a sigh. My Omega. My mate. My queen.

I sift my talons through her silky fire-stone hair and grip the back of her neck. Her collar bites my palm.

She might wear my collar, but she has leashed my heart.

I break the kiss, vowing, "I love you, Renee. I belong to you. Completely. Forever."

"As I am yours. No matter what happens."

I gaze at her, memorizing every detail of her beautiful face just inches from mine. A lilac crystal flutters down and settles on her long, dark lashes. She blinks. "Look! It's snowing."

A gust of freezing air blows us sideways. Straining to beat my wings against the force of it, I fly us towards a pocket of clean air. Plutus circles us, screeching.

Renee cranes her neck to look past my shoulder. "There! It looks like the lava is cooling."

A magical cold front is enveloping us, bringing clear, crisp winds to sweep away the ash, and coating the landscape with a lilac blanket of snow. Grey clouds sheath the volcano, freezing its fire in mid-blast.

We watch and wait for several tense moments, but no more lava erupts from Mount Vracor. The molten rock that oozed boiling crimson like a bleeding wound is rapidly healing over—first turning black, then smattered with pale purple as the freezing flakes continue to float from the sky.

The rumbling has stopped. All is still. Even Plutus has stopped screeching.

"Holy shit. It looks like it worked!" Renee beams up at me and I wipe the ash from her face, smearing it across her wind-chapped cheeks. With her eyes red-rimmed from the smoke, her lips plump from my ferocious kiss, she's never looked more beautiful.

"I believe it did." I wait another moment, marveling at the miracle taking place all around us. Soft snow continues to drift down, cooling the raging fires of Vracor—soothing the demon's heart. "The volcano is at peace. Pyreda is safe. And we are one."

"Then kiss me again," Renee says. "And take me home."

NINETEEN

Renee

RETURNING to the castle feels like coming home. I'm still reeling from everything that happened today but I can't stop grinning. Krav loves me. He finally opened up and let me in. We beat the volcano.

How quickly things can flip from utter despair to absolute joy. All I need now is to thaw out. I'm chilled to the bone.

A *jynx* appears as Krav is rubbing my hands by the fire, winding through the air like a diaphanous eel. For once, I didn't jump out of my skin. Things sure are looking up.

"Allow the villagers to spend the night," Krav tells the servant. "See to their every need. In the morning, provided Mount Vracor's fires have cooled completely, they may return home."

The *jynx* disappears with a swoosh.

Krav gets a pitcher and pours me a cup of *hima* juice to wash the dust from my throat. I gulp down the refreshing drink while he rolls his shoulders and slowly folds his wings.

"You brought the villagers here? Through the portal?"

Everything happened so fast when the ground started shaking.

"The ones from the settlement we visited today, closest to the volcano, yes. Evacuating them was the best option. They're in a suite of rooms on the ground floor here. While you were away, I tried to prevent Mount Vracor from erupting myself, but I wasn't strong enough. Not until you returned."

"You cared enough to do that?"

He conjures a wash basin and uses water and a cloth to wipe the worst of the ash from my face. I must look such a mess.

"They are my people. It was time I started behaving like their king."

"I'm glad you realized that."

"I realized a lot of things while you were gone."

His scent is intoxicating. I breathe him in, noting the subtle difference—the same bitter chocolate, but less smoke and more marshmallow. I want to lick him like a chocolate pop.

His tail curls around my leg and there's a long, languorous thump in my clit. I've missed his casually possessive gestures and the way he can make me melt with a single touch, or word.

"I realized some things too," I admit. "That you've never been in a relationship before, and the only model you had was that of your parents. In your way, you did try your best to care for me. I just got so flustered when you kept blowing hot and cold..."

"I was torn," he says. "Between what I wanted to do, and what I thought I *should* do. And I was confused. All my life, I've been told that demons don't feel. Don't love. So when I felt things here..." he reaches up and taps his chest over his heart, "I assumed they were yours. Your emotions, via the bond."

"Ah." *That makes a lot of sense.* I place my hand on his thigh, his hot skin warming my fingers as I trace the hard muscle. "I'll admit I was disappointed when you sent me the gifts. You've always given me things to keep me warm and brought me my favorite dishes." I shoot him a wink to take the sting out of my words. "Pampered your pet. But I wanted this." I twirl a finger in the air between us. "This connection. For you to love me as an equal—and treat me like one. When you said demons don't do love, I was heartbroken because I believed you. Because that meant we could never have the kind of relationship I wanted with you." The memory puts a lump in my throat and I swallow, fighting to keep my voice steady. "But I still had hope. When I watched you visit every village in your kingdom, and recognized you were recreating Christmas, it was clear you were trying to change. I still didn't know how you felt about me, but I figured, since you were taking my advice and reconnecting with your people, I could at least come and help."

"And you returned to me. Even though I'm a demon who rules over a hellscape. With a volcano threatening to erupt at any moment." He's grinning now, revealing that gorgeous dimple.

"I never said my life choices were always ideal," I say, but I'm smiling back at him. "Besides, we took care of that. Turns out we were strong enough together, just as you said. But I had no idea we could summon winter." If I'd known that becoming Krav's queen would give me Elsa-level powers, I might have pushed to claim the throne sooner. "Luckily, I dressed warmly. My Mrs. Claus outfit held up all right."

Looking down, I spot more ash on my bodice and dust it off. I'm in a garnet gown trimmed with white fur, an outfit Emma and I collaborated on. Both my new friends helped me come up with the best way to return and surprise Krav. Kim thought the whole thing was hilarious and kept singing,

Satan, Baby, put a tyrlee *under the tree...* until Emma threatened to take her drink away if she didn't stop.

Feeling Krav's gaze on me, I shoot him a seductive look. "Do you like it?"

Hunger darkens his mystic topaz eyes. "I like anything you wear. And I like it even better when you wear nothing."

In the glow of the dying embers, he looks especially monstrous. Firelight finds the hidden glow of his magenta skin, the rainbow colors in his eyes. Every part of him—from his talons to his fangs, his horns and tail, every muscle and sinew in his wings and massive body—was made to rule. To dominate. He's molded from volcanic fire, a creature of darkness.

He's silent, his gaze unfocused. Miles away.

"What are you thinking about?" I ask.

"How much I have to atone for. I'm so sorry, Renee. I see now how my actions hurt you, again and again. Before I was even old enough to mate, I vowed never to continue the demon line. I didn't want any child to grow up the way I did. If demons are unable to love, how could they be good parents? My father wrought nothing but fear and suffering on those around him. His mate, his son, his people—"

I take his hand. "I understand the thought process. But you are not your father, Krav."

"I know that now." His thumb is caressing my knuckles. "Which is why I'll stop preventing my seed from taking root in you. Provided you still want that?"

Unable to speak, dizzy with disbelief and burgeoning hope, I can only nod.

Krav's expression is everything. "I can't promise I'll be a perfect father," he says. "But once I allowed myself to picture it, I started getting more and more excited. And it would not only be a chance to prove I'm not like my father, but also to make amends, another way to show you that you are my mate, my equal, my queen. I want to give you everything your heart desires."

My sigh eases out of me. A burden that lay like a stone on my chest falls away. When I'm finally able to speak, my voice quivers. "We can take it one day at a time. It doesn't have to be right away."

"Now that I've made up my mind, I'm ready when you are," he says. "But you're right. We don't need to rush. We have forever. Thanks to you."

I beckon for him to lean down and he does. I pluck a silver strand from one of his horns, and trail my fingertips down the ribbed appendage. His shudder goes right through me.

He straightens and I shiver, even though we're in front of the fire. My skin feels tight, chapped from the alternating winter chill and volcanic heat.

"Are you cold, my love?" he asks.

"No. Just tired. And dirty."

"Then let me wash you. And put you to bed." He extends a talon-tipped hand and I don't miss the gleam in his eye, or the brief, tummy-twisting growl he lets out when I place my palm in his.

I'm exhausted but I want him to fuck me. I need to reconnect with him physically now we've got the emotional side of things sorted. Besides, it's been a hot minute. A girl has needs.

To my endless despair, Krav doesn't sex me up at all in the shower. He seems intent on proving how kind and gentle he can be. I'm luxuriating in it, but the wild side of me wants Krav the demon. My lover. My Master.

He washes the ash and soot from my skin and hair, and I examine the scorch marks on his wings. When the water's switched off and I've toweled myself dry, I turn to face him.

"I've been a very naughty girl." I put a hand on his massive chest, the heat searing my palm. "Maybe you should tie me up. Put a chain around my ankle."

His tail loops around my ankle and squeezes. He's solemn as he looms over me, there's darkness rising in his eyes. "I could keep you in a cage."

I suck in a breath.

"You'd like that, wouldn't you? To be bound and helpless, for me to use however I want," he rasps.

"I might. As long as you hold me afterwards. Master."

"Tut tut. Such a needy little pet." His chest rumbles with a growl, and the arousal hits me like a punch to the gut. Gasping, I splay a hand over his chest, caressing his plum-colored muscles. His skin is so hot to the touch, like a pot left to simmer on the stove.

"Master…" I moan, and he lifts me easily, carrying me into his bedroom. I'm plastered against his chest, his growl vibrating through every part of me. My own body heat is rising, my blood turning to lava.

"On the bed. All fours," he orders, setting me down. I scramble to obey. His tail spanks my ass and I arch my back, hoping to entice him to fuck me soon.

Instead, he runs his hands over me, as if checking me for injuries. He did this in the shower, too, but now it feels more intimate. Wrapping a handful of my wet hair around his fist, he pushes my upper body down on the bed.

"Look at you, naked and needy, splayed open for me," Krav murmurs, eliciting another surge of slick from my core.

His tail glides up the back of my left thigh and finds my clit, sliding back and forth between my labia with agonizing slowness. I groan.

"You'd better be a good girl for me." He spanks me hard enough to make me yelp at the sting. "No coming until I say so."

I dig my fingers into the sheets, fighting to obey him. My

whole body is straining, already on the edge. It's been so long since I've felt his touch.

"I'm tempted to paint this ass red. Mark you so you feel my punishment for days." He lets out a dark, sadistic chuckle. "I'd tease you the whole time, keeping you so close but never letting you go over, and then, when the last bruise fades… that's when you may have your release."

Why does that suggestion turn me on as much as it horrifies me? "I don't think I'd survive that, Master."

"You would. I know your body better than my own. I would keep you right on the edge…" His tail presses harder against my clit, and I gasp. "Maybe, if you please me, I will let you come today." He moves around me, positioning himself close to the bed and drawing me up by my hair to present his cock to my face. I close my eyes, open my mouth, and hum at the salty sweet taste of him.

His tail still delves into my lower folds as he fucks my throat. I rock my knees apart to invite the naughty appendage to fuck me. The tip of his tail dips into my pussy for a blissful second, then it draws out and plunges into my ass. I choke on Krav's dick, rolling my eyes up to look at him. He's got his *Master of the Universe but especially you* face on, his expression stern, his eyes whirling with colors. He seems to take pleasure in pushing forward until I've swallowed all of him, my lips wrapped around the base of his cock. Only his magic keeps me from gagging. His grip on my hair tightens, making tears spring into my eyes, but the hand on my cheek is gentle.

Cruel and gentle. Dominant and sweet. I open my jaw further and hum, sliding my tongue over the ridge on the underside of his shaft until his eyes roll back and he roars. His wings unfurl, straining to the ceiling.

With a groan, he guides me off his cock and up into his arms. I shiver as he winds a fist into my hair before covering my lips with his. His tongue fucks my mouth in the same rhythm as his tail thrusting in my ass.

I rock against him, needing friction against my throbbing clit.

He breaks the kiss. "Come for me, pet."

I'm still howling and contracting when he shifts, leaning back so he can set me on his cock. I'm dripping wet and I just came but it's still a stretch. I watch the hard, purple length impale me slowly. The aftershocks of my first orgasm haven't faded completely before the crests on his cock find the neediest spots inside of me and I come again. Lightning bolts of pleasure shoot through me. My clit is a live wire, sparking.

"There you go, that's a good girl, come nice and hard for me…"

"Master…"

"Come for me again. And this time, say my name."

I'm limp, boneless, seated completely on him like a puppet. My only movement is from his tail fucking my ass, and the friction is enough to send me flying.

"Krav…" My voice is barely audible as my climaxes crash over me. I writhe, impaled on him, stuffed full by his cock and his tail. I'm burning up in the fires of his eyes. My body is one long, undulating flame. I rise up in his lap, gripping his horns and dragging him down for another kiss. The bond between us rings with a Hallelujah chorus.

Krav moves, rising with his wings outstretched for balance. He grips my hips and raises me up only to slam me back down, splitting me in half. I explode like a volcano, hot liquid splashing the insides of my thighs.

He does it again. And again. Each thrust drives me to a new height of pleasure until I'm sobbing, half mindless.

I'm vaguely aware of him laying me down and moving over me, his sculpted face just inches away, his wild eyes intent on mine. He thrusts harder until his knot swells and he comes, his wings spread over us in a midnight canopy, kissing me on and on as he fills me with his release.

His knot is stretching me painfully and I wriggle until he gets the hint, sliding his tail out of me to relieve the pressure. I let out a little mewl as his beard chafes my cheeks.

With a contented sigh, he presses a kiss to my lips and wraps me in his arms, draping one wing protectively over me.

I close my eyes, exhausted and drained, but overflowing with love. The bond hums sweetly, a faint echo of the rumble in Krav's chest. It's reassuring to think his purr will always be with me, no matter where I am.

Not that I'm planning to leave ever again. I've got everything I want right here. Krav makes me feel safe, cherished, protected—and loved.

Who would have guessed I'd have to go to another freaking *planet* to find somewhere—and someone—that feels like home?

But now, I've finally arrived.

This is where I belong—right here, in my Demon King's arms.

And I intend to stay here forever.

ABOUT LEE SAVINO

Lee Savino is a USA today bestselling author of smexy romance. Smexy, as in "smart and sexy." Find her in the Goddess Group on facebook and download a free book at www.leesavino.com!

Find her at:
www.leesavino.com

Want more growly alphas? Check out the Berserker Saga. Start with <u>Sold to the Berserkers.</u>

Remember to download your free book at www. leesavino.com

The Berserker Saga

<u>Sold to the Berserkers</u> – Brenna, Samuel & Daegan
<u>Mated to the Berserkers -</u> – Brenna, Samuel & Daegan
<u>Bred by the Berserkers (FREE novella only available at www.leesavino.com) -</u> – Brenna, Samuel & Daegan
<u>Taken by the Berserkers</u> – Sabine, Ragnvald & Maddox
<u>Given to the Berserkers</u> – Muriel and her mates
Claimed by the Berserkers – Fleur and her mates

Ménage Sci Fi Romance

Draekons (Dragons in Exile) with Lili Zander (ménage alien dragons)

Crashed spaceship. Prison planet. Two big, hulking, bronzed aliens who turn into dragons. The best part? The dragons insist I'm their mate.

Paranormal romance

Bad Boy Alphas with Renee Rose (bad boy werewolves)
Never ever date a werewolf.

Possessive Warrior Sci-fi romance

Draekon Rebel Force with Lili Zander
Start with Draekon Warrior

Tsenturion Warriors with Golden Angel
Start with Alien Captive

Contemporary Romance

Royal Bad Boy
I'm not falling in love with my arrogant, annoying, sex god boss. Nope. No way.

Royally Fake Fiancé
The Duke of New Arcadia has an image problem only a fiancé can fix. And I'm the lucky lady he's chosen to play Cinderella.

Beauty & The Lumberjacks
After this logging season, I'm giving up sex. For...reasons.

Her Marine Daddy
My hot Marine hero wants me to call him Daddy...

Her Dueling Daddies
Two daddies are better than one.

Innocence: dark mafia romance with Stasia Black
I'm the king of the criminal underworld. I always get what I want. And she is my obsession.

Beauty's Beast: a dark romance with Stasia Black
Years ago, Daphne's father stole from me. Now it's time for her to pay her family's debt...with her body.

ABOUT TABITHA BLACK

Want more seriously hot, dark, sci-fi romance? Get your
FREE book here: Rescued Mate

I love to write in different genres but my books all have one
thing in common: incandescent passion.

Dominant, dirty-talking heroes are my weakness, and I'm so
lucky I get to discover the heroes of my dreams as I write -
and then share them with you!

I just adore getting feedback, so if you want to drop me a
line, please do so at:
tabitha@incandescentpassion.com.

If you want to hear about my new releases and projects,
please feel free to to sign up for my newsletter, follow me on
BookBub, or Amazon, and/or join my Shameless Readers on
Facebook.

Thank you for reading!

Don't miss these other exciting books by Tabitha!

Paranormal

Planet of Kings - With Lee Savino
Brutal Mate - Book 1
Brutal Claim - Book 2

Brutal Capture - Book 3
Brutal Beast - Book 4
Brutal Demon - Book 5

Warrior Kings - box set PoK 1-3

Alphas of Sandor (Omegaverse)
Primal Possession - Book 1
Primal Mate - Book 2

Midnight Doms (BDSM)
Her Vampire Addiction

Contemporary BDSM

His Empire Series
Restraint - Book 1
Denial - Book 2
Anticipation - Novella

Masters of the Castle Series
Fulfilling Her Fantasy
Sharing Silver
Tempting Tasha
Undoing Una

Anthologies
When the Gavel Falls (Sharing Silver)
Witness Protection Program (Tempting Tasha)
Dominating His Valentine (Anticipation)
Daddies of the Castle (Undoing Una)

Audiobooks
Little Tudor Rose
Conquering Cassia

Restraint
Sapphire's Surrender
Primal Possession